The Curators

A "Humanity, Fuck Yeah!" Sci-Fi Space Opera
by
Roger Williams
☼☼☼

The universe is a garden carefully cultivated by the billions-year-old species known as The Curators. Everything is under control.

Then an obscure species from a small blue planet pops up—and nothing will ever be the same.

The 29 chapters of this 50,000-word space opera were originally published online to the "Humanity, Fuck Yeah!" subreddit. We now offer it in paperback for the very first time.

Copyright & Credits

All Rights Reserved
Text © 2017, 2018 Roger Williams
Cover Design by Peachfront Press

⟨ ⟩

EXCEPT FOR BRIEF PASSAGES quoted for reviews and/or recommendations in magazine, radio, or blog posts, no part of this book may be reproduced in any form or by any means, electronic or mechanical, including photocopying or recording, or by information storage or retrieval system, without permission in writing from the author.

This book is a work of fiction and any resemblance to anyone, any time, or any place is not intended and is merely coincidental. The cover model appears for illustration purposes only and has no relationship to any events in this story. Brief mentions of real persons, places, or products are used fictitiously and in accordance with fair use. All trademarks remain the properties of their owners.

Although you are perfectly welcome to read this story for free online at the "Humanity, Fuck Yeah!" subreddit, the author has retained all rights to this work. Do not upload it for free to other sharing sites or sell it anywhere as your own work.

Episode 1

It had been three years since the foldship appeared in our sky, and I was a bit amazed to find one of our alien visitors on my appointment book. The aliens could travel between the stars but had a very limited ability to move between their orbiting ship and the Earth's surface, so we had brought them a docking ring and with their help affixed it to their ship so that we could do shuttle service. There were thousands of individuals of several races from different star systems on their ship but only a handful had actually made it to the Earth's surface, and now one of them was sitting across my desk from me and I had no idea why.

"I'm honored and puzzled," I said.

"You are your world's foremost expert on patterns that emerge on the dermis of your species," it said. My visitor was bipedal but had a chitonous exoskeleton and didn't wear clothes. Its color changed according to its mood; at the moment it was bright blue. It spoke through an electronic translator that mimicked human inflections pretty well. And I had no idea what gender it was, or even whether our idea of gender might make any sense to it.

"I study diseases of the skin," I said. "Birthmarks are also part of my work."

THE CURATORS

"I am seeking the Mark of the Curators."

"None of your people have ever said anything about this."

"If I may?" I made my terminal available and my visitor navigated to a diagram of two equilateral triangles arranged point-to-point. "This diagram appears somewhere on the dermis of every multicellular species the Curators have affected." He arranged a slideshow which quickly showed me the same design in colors on skin, colored or missing hair, colored or missing scales, and colored and differently textured chitin. "If I may," it said, and it stood and turned around, bowing slightly. There was the pattern, about six centimeters across and horizontal about at the point a human would call the small of its back.

"I can't say I've ever seen that," I said.

"This is remarkable. I have observed the Mark of the Curators on thousands of individuals of hundreds of species, and shared records of its occurrence of hundreds of thousands of species with my fellow researchers."

"What is its incidence?"

"For intelligent species, it is one hundred percent. I have to ask if your species' modesty habit might be hiding it for some reason. I assure you I have no prurient interest in your reproductive apparatus."

I sighed heavily. This was certainly not something I'd anticipated in medical school, but I moved to the open floor and disrobed. The alien examined my body with the attention a lover might show, but a growing agitation that was anything but amorous. Its exoskeleton slowly turned green as its puzzlement increased.

"This is remarkable," it finally said, for the first time sitting down. "I have studied the Curators for my entire career, and to my knowledge nobody has ever encountered a member of a species with language much less space travel that does not have the Mark."

"Maybe it would help if you told me something about these Curators. I have no idea what you are talking about," I said as I put my clothes back on.

"That is also remarkable. Every sapient species we know of has known of the Curators."

"Well I can assure you we don't. I'm pretty well educated by human standards and I think I'd know if we did."

"The Curators are vastly powerful and they love carbon-based intelligent life. They do not intervene often in the path of any particular world, but when they do as far as we know their powers have no limit. When they find a lifeless world or proto-world with promise, they intervene to improve its chances of becoming life-bearing. When they find a barren but habitable world, they introduce simple microbic life. When they find a world where microscopic life has increased in complexity and remade the environment, they make sure it becomes multicellular. When they find a world where multicellular life has become complex enough to support intelligence, they insert key genomic factors to encourage that. When they find a world with life capable of understanding, they encourage the development of technology. But they also mark what they have altered. I suppose I shall have to find a geneticist. There is also a genomic mark which is less likely to degrade via evolution."

"As a doctor, I have access to the genomic library," I said. "What is it you are looking for?"

It gave me a sequence of about a hundred base pairs, and I ran the search. "This doesn't occur anywhere, nor does any sub-part of it more than twenty pairs long."

The alien became even more agitated. "This is truly remarkable," it said. Its color began to turn from green to dark violet.

"Perhaps these curators simply never came to Earth."

"Oh no, they certainly did. The formation of your Moon which helpfully stabilises its axis of rotation? Almost certainly them. The occurrence of such large satellites around planets of this type is almost twenty times what might be expected by chance. Your Cambrian Explosion, also Curators. Such an event has happened on every world we know of with multicellular life, and in many cases it is marked. Other possiblities are in the record, but also most likely your K-T impactor which ended the era of the animals you call dinosaurs."

"Wait, if these Curators love life so much why would they hit our world with an asteroid and almost wipe out all life?"

"They don't love life. They love *intelligent* life. Your fossil explorations draw a detailed picture—your archaeologists are among the best I've ever encountered. Life on Earth had stagnated in a stable pattern for tens of millions of years, with ravenous monsters dominating the most productive continents. The Curators are known to intervene in this way in such cases. They left the coast clear so your ancestors could evolve into you."

"If they love intelligent life so much and they're so powerful, why don't they just make it from scratch?"

"We don't know. That is a great mystery all of our races have pondered for literally millions of your years. We think they want to encourage, not create, and be surprised by what arises. So they create favorable conditions, but they do not directly create what they want."

"So how do they intervene to encourage technology?"

"They leave gifts. Papers, drawings, artifacts. Every species has its tales of the mysterious package that gave the idea for steam power, or electric power distribution, or the fold interstellar transport. In fact that's an interesting thing; we found your world because we detected an anomalous fold pattern, which we thought might be the signature of a fold ship in peril, but it turned out you were just commencing research and doing experiments. You hadn't had a gift to guide you. We've been helping your scientists finish the..."

"Maybe we just did it ourselves without their help."

"I don't believe that has ever happened before," the alien said.

"Well, everything has to happen for a first time."

Episode 2

When I decided to study dermatology I never dreamed it would result in my becoming an astronaut, much less visiting actual aliens on their starship. But the foldship was now getting closer and closer and bigger and bigger through the windows of the personnel shuttle and when I finally spotted the docking ring humans had given them it was like a wedding ring lost on the side of a mountain.

I had been told there were fifteen hundred individuals of twenty-two species on the ship, and they were all manner of scaly, furry, feathered, and naked. The human habit of wearing clothes didn't seem to be a big thing off-Earth and was a source of some curiosity among our hosts. My primary host, the researcher I call K because I can't pronounce any of the alien names, allowed as to how there were some species who had what he called deviant modesty habits here and there in the galaxy. It was a primary suspicion of it that we were hiding our Marks of the Curator for some reason until I allowed it to inspect my dermis thoroughly. Fortunately it shared my values as a doctor and was as courteous as it could be despite its agitation.

The ship wasn't spinning but it had some kind of local interior gravity. I guess we hadn't got that memo yet from the Curators either.

There were a few other scientists on the shuttle but most of the passengers were diplomats. The aliens seemed quite puzzled that we had no single world authority they could correspond with. For practical reasons their worlds all had different governments, and of many different forms and philosophies, but each of their worlds tended to be unified. Our guys reminded them that we are a very young species by their standards, having only mastered steam travel a couple of hundred years ago. They seemed astonished that we had gotten into space so quickly after that. Apparently the Curators don't pass out the gifts quite that often.

Finally I was in a stateroom which had been furnished to a pretty decadent human standard. Apparently there were dozens of architects and living space designers on their crew, and our world had presented them with a new pallette of playthings. The distilled liquor I requested was indistinguishable from Jack Daniel's even though I knew they had synthesized it on the ship. "We didn't need a very large sample, and when we knew you favored it we had one of the other guests bring us a few drops to analyze," K told me.

"I still don't know why I'm here," I said as I sipped my Jack D. while lounging in a bathrobe in my decadent starship stateroom.

"You know your species' skin better than anybody, and it is the mark of the Curators we seek," K said.

"I thought we had pretty well established that the Curators haven't marked humans, and don't seem to have done anything

THE CURATORS

noticeable on Earth since the unfortunate ex-dinosaur business."

"That seems likely, but my colleagues will need more evidence before they believe that."

I sighed heavily, imagining myself doing the disrobing and examination thing in an auditorium. The sacrifices we make for knowledge.

The lights turned red and started blinking. "What the hell is this?" I asked.

"Oh, the foldship is leaving Earth," K said.

"And when is it coming back?" I asked with a bit of bite in my voice. I had just meant to visit the ship, not to leave the Solar System with it.

"It will come back when it is appropriate." And as I watched through the window the image of the Earth became dim, as though seen through a grey filter, until it was barely visible. Then there was an impossibly bright flash of light, and when my vision recovered I was looking at an alien starfield and a gas giant planet.

"Surely nobody lives there," I said. It was dimly lit and it seemed likely that even a moon couldn't possibly get enough sunlight to harbor life.

"No, we will perform a few fold maneuvers in the gas planet's gravitational field to adjust our local velocity before folding over to our host world. We did the same thing when we arrived at Sol, using the gravity of your solar world Neptune to match velocity with your Earth."

"Wait, if you can fold the ship from the bottom of a gravity well out of it, doesn't that make the fold drive a perpetual motion machine?"

"Yes, it violates your so-called 'first law of thermodynamics.' We create energy to power the ship and our cities using similar principles."

"This is going to drive our physicists nuts."

"A failure to accept it was part of your physicists' problem creating your own fold drive. Now that we have proven it is possible they are well on their way to success."

Five Earth days later we were orbiting a blue world, one which was Earthlike but also very obviously not Earth. The shuttles which came to ferry us to the surface were powered by some kind of field projected from the surface; this was also used to launch the components to be assembled into large structures like the foldship itself. But the generator required a local gravity well to work and so could not be used in space, which is why we humans had to provide ferry service at Earth. I learned that our hosts were quite bemused at our use of chemical rockets, which they had never bothered to develop to such a high degree.

"If you don't mind I'd like to take a sample of your flesh so that we can sequence your genome ourselves," K said. "It's not that we don't trust you or your skills, but the idea that you've been untouched by the Curators is going to be very hard for some of us to believe and it would make a better case if we used methods we know."

I allowed blood and saliva samples to be taken and a detailed photographic survey to be taken of my skin. Most of the other humans on board were diplomats and engineers and I verified that human modesty habits would make them bristle at similar requests.

THE CURATORS

The following day K and I took the shuttle to the surface and visited the genetics lab. It took about an hour for them to sequence my genome, and as the results unfolded the operator of the sequencing machine changed hue until it was a spectacular bright green. "This is quite remarkable," it kept saying.

"Can you explain just how?"

"Your genome does contain fragments of Curator marks," it said. "But they are highly mutated. It has been hundreds of thousands of generations since the Curators touched your ancestors. The last thing I can be fairly sure they did was making your ancestors omnivorous."

"That was probably a few million years ago," I said.

"Exactly, and yet you have language, civilization, architecture, and *space travel*. Clearly all without their help. This is unprecedented."

"Just how do you tell? Remember that we've never seen any of these gifts so we don't know what you're looking for."

K turned dark red. "Of course. We simply hadn't thought of that. Let's go to the museum."

The same generator that powered space shuttles powered flying ground transports, so the aliens had what were basically flying cars. They were also automatic and self-navigating, and shared in some kind of public system. We were at the museum which was half a continent away in about an hour. K produced a set of what looked oddly like eyeglasses. "I had these made to your species' form factor," K said. "They should make it possible for you to interpret the exhibits."

I put them on and looked at the front of the building; the indecipherable squiggle above the door suddenly said "Museum of Curator Artifacts." We went inside.

"We can skip the early exhibits, which are about the development of habitable worlds and life, since we are pretty sure the Curators did do those things on Earth." Toward the back of the building we reached an exhibit with a large flat rock covered with diagrams, and inlaid with gemstones. At the center was some kind of agate that glowed red. The sign called this a "Prometheus Stone."

"This was the gift of how to make fire for some ancient people," K said. "This one is a replica; they are given to very primitive races so most have been lost or destroyed even though the gift of fire itself remained. Only four of the genuine article are known to exist in the galaxy. It is quite possible there is one on Earth, or was once, because it seems to be associated with the diet-widening modification you were given."

"Our ancestors were herbivorous and couldn't eat meat until we learned to cook it," I said. "Fire and omnivorism are thought to be closely linked for us. But it is also thought that we may have spent a long period of time harvesting fire from natural sources like lightning strikes before we learned to make it from scratch." The Prometheus Stone illustrations showed the making and use of a fire drill, a method human adventurers still use to make fire under primitive conditions.

I spent two days going through the museum. The aliens were quite obsessed with the details of their gifts and had learned a lot about how the Curators had helped them, if very little about the Curators themselves or their ultimate motivations.

"The foldship will soon return to Earth, but I would like to suggest an alternate destination for you," K said. "There is another foldship we can take to *scree* which is the homeworld of another relatively young race. They are still doing archaeology and it would give you a chance to see some actual Curator artifacts and meet people who are doing current research on the Curators. They would probably also like to meet a member of your species, given your remarkable lack of Curation."

I could think of a hundred reasons why it was a bad idea, but in the end I couldn't resist. All the diplomats and engineers returned to Earth, but I became the first of my species to visit two alien worlds.

Episode 3

K brought me to the dig site and introduced me to the alien leading the excavation. My great-aunt was an archaeologist and I had visited her dig sites as a child, so much of the work was familiar. Unlike K's species these aliens were more like Earth mammals, snouted and furry. But the aliens working the site had all shaved themselves bare. Their Mark of the Curators was right above their genitals, and quite prominent when they were shaved.

Several of the scientists made time to visit when K told them where I was from. "It is amazing to meet a specimen of a species so untouched by the Curators," he said with a slight bow.

"We aren't entirely untouched by them. Apparently they used their usual methods to make our world habitable and encourage early life, but after changing us from herbivores to omnivores they apparently didn't do anything else."

"Remarkable. Just remarkable."

"And what are you investigating here?"

"Oh, we are fairly certain this is the place where the Curators gave us writing. The site is well preserved because it was buried by a volcanic eruption *screee* ago, and we are hoping to find the Tablet. If it still exists it will be one of about a hundred known to exist in the galaxy."

"The translator didn't get the time frame."

K consulted a tablet computer. "Eight hundred thousand of your years," it said.

"Wow, our modern-form species is only about a hundred and thirty thousand years old." The scientist looked at K, and K said something to the tablet which said something in a language that sounded like a thousand weiner dogs yapping for dinner. "Oh, that is remarkably short. And without help or hints! Remarkable!"

"It took us almost a million years to move from writing to space travel on *screee*," K said.

"This translator not doing names business is getting annoying."

"Well translators need to be told what to call things in your language. Apparently nobody has given our world a human name. What would you call it?"

"Well you came on a voyage of discovery and discovered us, so how about Seville. That is where the first voyage to circumnavigate the Earth started."

"Fitting!" said the lead archaeologist. "Pick one for our world!"

"What would you consider your world special for?"

"Our world isn't particularly special. We are a young race by the standards of the galaxy, though obviously not as young as you humans. We do seem to have a high number of preserved artifacts, ironically because volcanism frequently buries them."

"If you don't find it too gruesome then I will call your world Pompeii. That is a human city that was buried by a volcano two thousand years ago. Unfortunate for the humans who lived there, but we learned a great deal digging them up."

"You had to do archeaology to learn about people who practically lived yesterday," he said. "Your species does move fast. We will carry your name Pompeii with honor."

What I didn't know at the time was that the alien computers are all interconnected through periodic Fold transactions, and my names were distributed throughout the galaxy within a few weeks. I also started a somewhat annoying trend of other people naming alien worlds after human cities. But I had to call them *something* and the human habit of letting the first human visitor name a place persisted.

"Just what would this Tablet look like if you find it?" I asked.

K offered the use of his own tablet. "Of the Tablets known to exist, about five still function," the archaeologist said. "They were active devices which would talk to you when you touched symbols." He showed me the screen. The Tablet resembled a flat stone but functioned much like a tablet computer. In low frame rate video the hand of yet another species of alien was touching symbols which indeed made the thing squawk like a parrot.

"It's a Speak-and-Spell," I said.

"The translator did not like that," K and the scientist said together.

"An early human computer product. Very primitive by our standards today but we used them to teach our children to write correctly."

"You build things like this yourselves? Without nanites from the Curators?"

"Nanites?"

"All of our microscopic machines are made by them. We don't actually know how the Curators originally made them, but we know how to use them and make them make more of their own kind."

The Sevillian foldship had been at Earth for three years and this was something we apparently had not learned about the aliens' technology. Or if we had our leaders had not bothered to share it with the general population.

"Some of our futurists have speculated on the possibility of nanites, but we haven't learned to make our own. We make computers by direct manufacturing."

"But how?"

"Sorry but I'm a doctor, not an engineer. I understand that it somehow involves etching patterns on the surface of silicon wafers, but I really have no idea how it works."

After we left, K plied me with a fifth of Johnny Walker Blue, a luxury I could not afford in Earth's decidedly non-post-scarcity economy. "We did not know you could make electronics from scratch," it said. "Your negotiators seem to have forgotten to mention that."

"Did you tell them that you can't make your own without the Curators' nanites?"

"Of course, we take it for granted that's true of *everybody*."

"Well, they may have feared you would think it dangerous knowledge."

"Considering they were developing a fold drive, and an improperly configured fold drive can fold your world into its host star by accident, I can't imagine what they would find dangerous about..."

I sprayed a very expensive shot of scotch across the room. "A fold drive can do *WHAT*?"

"It can destroy a world. Isn't it obvious? The fold drive folds spacetime so that distant points touch and matter and energy can cross over. The two most obvious nearby peaks when you are working on a habitable world are the center of the world itself, and then of the star it orbits. Moving a habitable world to the center of a star tends to ruin its habitability."

"Do our people know this?"

"The ones working on the drive do, now that we have told them. My understanding is that they had already figured out the danger themselves and were exercising proper care."

"And this is general knowledge around the Galaxy?"

"Of course. One reason we diverted to visit you was a bit of worry that you might do something unfortunate by accident. It's a fate many races warn their young of to shock them into acting more responsibly."

"Has it ever happened?"

"The Curators are explicit with their warnings when they give us the fold drive, so it's very rare, but some races have turned out to be a bit careless," K said.

"I think I need to get back to Earth," I said a bit shakily.

"The foldship *screee* returns to Seville in about six Earth days. At that point my foldship *screee* will probably already be present and should return to Earth with new researchers within an Earth lunar cycle."

While I was waiting to depart Seville, the news arrived that the Pompeiian archaeologists had found their Tablet of Writing. Unfortunately, having been buried by a pyroclastic flow, it would not be one of the few that were still operational.

Meanwhile, I needed to have a word with the people developing our human fold drive. It was a word our new friends didn't seem to know, and one I was now very afraid to say around them— *weapon*.

Episode 4

The Foldship project was of course one of the most important and high-security projects in human history, but I was the only human to make the side trip to the world I had called Pompeii and the opportunity to debrief me about that was enough to get me an appointment with the project director.

He didn't seem to find much that I said surprising, although I was surprised that he called the world I had visited "Pompeii." "Oh, somebody seems to have given them some names," he said in a tone half way between jovial and sneering.

"It was just a shorthand for the translator," I said.

"So you obviously thought at the time. What you didn't realize is those little tablets they have aren't very smart. They can't play what we would consider proper video, and they only have a few megabytes of local storage. They are completely dependent on a microfold link to a data processing center on their homeworld to do anything useful. Since they have as much energy as they want from fold technology those centers are enormous—cubic miles in extent. Every inhabited world in the galaxy has several."

"Wait, what, they are in real-time communication across light-years?"

"Amazing, isn't it. For computers comparable to something we would have made in 1990."

"But they've been spacefaring for hundreds of thousands of years."

"Yes, but they've also been Curated. They were given nanites. That makes it so easy for them to build what they have, the effort to go beyond what the nanites can do never seems to have been invested."

"I have to ask you something. My friend K told me that a fold drive can destroy a planet."

"It was telling the truth. Our new friends don't seem to do guile well."

"And our people knew this?"

"Of course. There are three fundamental constants which determine the extent and range of the fold effect, and there is no way to find out what they are except to make a fold. And if you get them wrong, it will fold the two nearest large masses together. Which is why we made our first experimental foldship a robotic interplanetary probe and did our first experiments from the Mars-Solar Langrange 3 point when Earth was on the far side of the Sun from Mars. Since we didn't know the constants our first experiments were unbalanced, and this is what our friends detected before they moved to save us from our folly."

"How close did we come to annihilation?"

"Give us some credit. We might have folded Mars into the Sun, but even that was very unlikely. And we would have figured the constants out for ourselves within a year. Our experimental protocol was on track when our new friends surprised us by arriving."

"K said they use the danger to warn their young to be responsible."

"Yes, not a bad idea. But the Curators give them the values for the constants. None of them have ever had to exercise caution to learn them the hard way, at risk."

"K said some species were still, as it said, careless."

"Well you can't cure stupid."

"Stupid normally can't destroy a planet."

"Stupid can destroy more than you realize. Ever study World War One?"

"Okay, but has it ever occurred to anybody to make this thing into a weapon instead of a travel device?"

"Fancy a drink?" The Director produced a bottle of 1800 Scotch from a desk drawer and I nodded somberly. "Of course we have," he said as he poured me a straight shot. "We also asked as closely as we dared if our alien friends had ever done so. The answer in every context was no. Making a foldship into a planet-killer also makes it a suicide run, because the foldship also folds itself into the star."

"So it can't be used that way?"

"I didn't say that. As with their less than stellar computing devices none of them seem to have autonomous probes with fold drives. Their fold ships need sentient guidance to operate, and they also don't seem to have the concept of suicide as triumph."

"And our very first fold ship is an autonomous probe," I said.

The Director held up his shot glass, and I joined him in a rather morbid salute to my species.

"Just how easy is it to make a fold drive?" I asked. "Some of our fellow humans would fold us into the Sun just for spite."

"It's far too easy if you have the nanites and the programming system, which is common on their worlds. We have told the aliens we are afraid of what the Curators might do if they find that we've been given that technology, but we're really more afraid of our own people getting it. We're also not planning to duplicate their ground to orbit technology any time soon for similar reasons. Fortunately they don't have much of an answer for ground to orbit if there isn't a fold-based ground infrastructure waiting for them, and making them rely on our chemical rockets gives us a bit of a barrier."

"Wait a minute, how do they deal with new worlds then?"

The Director poured himself another shot, offered, and I accepted. "There are really no new worlds for these guys," he said as he tossed it back. "The worlds they discover have been Curated and have transport networks, as the Curators intended. They don't seek out uninhabited or primitive worlds and wouldn't know what to do with one if they stumbled across it."

"I think I need to get back to my practice," I said as the scotch began to make its effect known.

"Oh, I don't think that would be a very good idea. Your clinic is in the middle of an excellent path for a new highway and the eminent domain papers are ready to be delivered."

"What?"

"We don't know shit about this galaxy we find ourselves living in, and you have an inside track to learn more. Investigate this 'Mark of the Curators' with your friend K. We will pay you fabulously well. It is one of the few things our mostly incurious new friends are very curious about. And frankly, we are pretty curious here too. You see, it's not the races the Curators have groomed that we fear. They have all settled at a tech level we think we can match in a few decades, and have already exceeded in some areas. Beyond our worry about what our own assholes would do with their technology, it's the Curators themselves that we fear. We don't know why they Curate, and we don't know why they didn't Curate us. We don't know the extent of their power. They are obviously active in the present day and we don't know what they might do when they realize we have appeared on the galactic stage."

"I'm just a dermatologist," I protested. "You want me to suddenly be James Bond?"

"Oh, we want you to be far more than just James Bond. Bond didn't have to deal with a galaxy full of alien species. Hell, he only went into low Earth orbit once in the movies. You've already visited and named two alien worlds orbiting other stars. And it turns out you are just what your species needs, because it is a mark on the skin that is at the core of all of this. We don't know anything about the Curators, and we don't know much about the few aliens we've met, but we know a lot about ourselves, and we know that even though we weren't Curated we come from the same basic Curator tree of life they do. And one thing I know about humans is that when we put a mark on something it's often because we think we own it."

So it was that a week later I was on another rocket shuttle, headed back to K's foldship and the world I had named Seville. But this time I did something that was expressly forbidden in the densely worded contract I had once signed.

I loaded up some carefully selected apps and files and packed my cellphone and a solar charger.

Episode 5

While we were still falling through the gravity well of one of the Seville system's gas giants in order to match velocity for Seville orbit, I invited K to my stateroom and showed it the phone. "You asked me a question on my last visit and I wasn't able to answer," I said. "This time I brought the answer." I navigated to the phone's video gallery and queued up a documentary on the manufacture of modern integrated circuits.

K's dermis was brown when the video started but slowly turned dark red, then bright red, as it watched. K made a gesture and I demonstrated the touch control to pause the playback.

"How is this thing getting video data from Earth?"

"It isn't. It's self-contained."

"You have an *entire video* stored in a device this size?"

"It's much worse than that. I flipped the phone over and popped the cover, revealing the memory chip the size of a human fingernail. "This video, and about a hundred more, are stored in *that*."

"How in the cosmos is this possible?"

"The video you are watching explains that."

K started watching again. Silicon plates were cut, polished, vacuum deposited, exposed, etched, rinsed. And then it was done again, with slightly different chemicals. And again. And again. K paused the video.

"How accurately do these things have to be registered each time they put them back in the vacuum chamber?"

"It's in the video intro, but I think this is a twenty nanometer process. So quite a bit less than that, obviously. They use optical methods, in this case with ultraviolet light to keep the wavelength as short as possible."

"And they do this how many times?"

"The video explains it. I think there are about thirty steps in this process."

"AND THIS WORKS?"

"You are holding the result in your hands."

K finished the video, its dermis almost glowing flourescent green by the time it was done. "How many of these machines can your species produce?"

"Just about every one of us gets a new one every year or two as they improve."

"But that means you must make billions of them, by this convoluted and insane process!"

"And we do just that. The plant where those chips are made cost over a billion dollars to build, and it's just one of many that are necessary to make these devices."

"The penalty did not translate."

I thought about it a bit. "It represents the directed effort of tens of thousands of humans, focused on nothing else, for at least a year."

I recognized that it was K's turn to be thoughtful. "How on Earth do you get your people to put in that kind of effort to make things like this?"

"We give them tokens which they can exchange for things like this, called 'money.' You need money for other things which your people seem to take for granted, so my people are motivated to do what they can to get a supply. K, I know you were one of the negotiators dealing most frequently with my people, didn't we tell you about any of this?"

"No. Nothing like this. Nothing about this system you have ... do you mean that basic life necessities like food and water are tied to this 'money' system?"

I nodded, a gesture I knew K understood. "We call it capitalism. It's been pretty successful."

"It sounds distressingly coercive."

"Well, truthfully, it is. But nobody gave us the gifts your people got, so we had to come up with something. Come to think of it, I have no idea where your technology comes from either."

"We hid nothing from your people. We assumed your leaders would inform you."

"On Earth that's not always a good assumption. I've shown you mine K, how can I learn about your technology?"

"I know exactly who you need to talk to."

Two days later the foldship had made orbit, the shuttle had taken us to the surface, and K was introducing me to one of Seville's top nanite assembly researchers. The walls of the office were lined with what seemed to be electron micrographs. We started the meeting by letting it watch the video on my phone.

"This is remarkable," it said. "K has alerted me to this device's prodigous memory capacity, but how is it powered?"

"Chemical battery," I said. I popped the cover and showed it. "It's dying though, at about fifty percent capacity. I brought a device which can recharge it but it needs a source of very bright light, like sunshine."

"Oh, we can accommodate you for that," the researcher said. "It has never occurred to anyone in millions of years to try anything like the production effort this video portrays. The number of ways for things to go wrong would simply be seen as silly, and using nanites is so much easier."

"I brought him here so he can see our methods," K said.

"Ah. Well, behold." It led me to one of the wall posters and tapped it. "This is a single nanite, possibly the greatest gift of the Curators since we became sapient." It was a cube with some patterns on its sides.

"Is that an electron micrograph? How big is it?"

After some dickering with the translator we established that yes, it was a scanning electron micrograph, and the nanite was about four hundred nanometers on edge. "A single nanite isn't good for much though," the researcher said. "Here is the simplest structure we know of which can create more nanites. It consists of about five hundred nanites itself, and it doesn't actually do anything with the nanites it creates, although other processes can use them."

"What does it use as raw materials?"

"Ultraviolet light for energy, silicon dioxide which it separates into oxygen and silicon, and trace elements dissolved in a surrounding fluid. It's not hard to arrange. Our immature young are encouraged to make a nanite nursery as part of their education."

"And what can they do?"

"They can be electronic amplifying or digital computation elements, or structural elements. They can store electrical energy and emit light. Practical assemblies require hundreds of thousands, millions, or even more nanites, but arbitrarily large numbers of them can be self-assembled from simple materials as part of a larger construction process. Most of our buildings are made of them, since it's so much easier to let the building build itself than to maneuver heavy materials into place."

I had noticed that for all their high tech, neither Seville nor Pompeii had buildings higher than ten or fifteen stories. "What's the tensile strength of a block of nanites?"

After more dickering with the translator we established it was about four thousand PSI. "Our structural steel is about ten times stronger than that," I said.

"But what do you have to do to make it?"

"We melt it."

"What's it made of?"

"Iron and nickel." I had been thinking of information technology and had not thought to bring a video of a foundry or steel mill.

"You *melt metals* in quantities large enough to make a *building*?"

"All the time."

"I suppose this takes the directed coordination of thousands of humans too?"

"Yes, that's kind of how we do everything. Surely you have things that aren't made of nanites?"

"Well, obviously we can't eat them but much of our agriculture is run by machines that are made of them. They are capable of precise positioning and selective chemical selection so we can use them to make plastics and other chemicals, and we use those for most things nanites are a bit rough or overkill for, such as pipes and utensils."

"Tell me something. Your young can make nanites, can they make advanced things with them?"

"If they want to. The designs are openly available."

"What about the fold drive?"

"Well of course, it's made of nanites. It takes a lot of them but it's not hard to get a lot of nanites. Of course there's not much point making a fold drive on the surface of the planet since you'd fold off a pretty big crater if you tried to use it."

"And the fold drive can fold your world into its star by accident."

"Well the Curators gave us the configuration constants, so there's no danger of that for us."

"What if someone decided to do it deliberately?"

"Well nobody would do that because it would be suicide."

I decided that was probably a good place to say "Okay, thanks," and end the conversation. There were obviously a *lot* of things my fellow humans had not told these folks about us.

Later K presented at my door with a container of something called Royal Salute, which turned out to be another stupidly expensive Scotch they could easily duplicate from a few sample drops. "You are hiding something," K accused correctly.

"You've learned a lot about us," I said trying to deflect.

"You're trying to deflect," K said.

Dealing with totally honest people is really a strange but also addictive thing. "Some of my people would deliberately use the fold drive to kill us all," I said."

"Oh, we've known that for a few years."

"It doesn't seem like anyone I've dealt with except you knows this."

"We really don't know what to do about it, and it is kind of terrifying. Many of your people are brilliant and noble but many others are very ill."

I nodded gravely. "Maybe we should blame the Curators for ignoring us."

K held up its glass in the gesture it had learned from me. I met it with mine and clinked. "We have no idea why you were denied," K said, "but everyone among us thinks it was wrong. It has left you with challenges we cannot imagine—and you have met those challenges with solutions we could not imagine either."

"That will be a great thing to know if humanity survives this."

"It is not your race I worry about," K said to my surprise. "I am what your people call a 'diplomat.' I have traveled the galaxy and met members of thousands of species. We all have the same nanites, the same fold drive, the same moon stabilizing our world. We all breathe oxygen and are built by DNA. As different as our species are, you and I share at least fifty percent the same DNA because of the Curators." K tossed back its drink, and I realized it had been drinking quite a bit before it came to my room.

"Are you all right?" I asked.

"I don't think any of us are all right right now," K replied. "As far as we have always known nanites and the fold drive are the peak achievements of technology. This has been the case for close to eight billion of your Earth years. We have no idea what the Curators might have held out on us. After all, they must have somehow made the first few nanites. I never really thought about that much until you showed me the fabrication video. At some point the Curators must have been like you. After all, nobody Curated them either."

K kicked back its drink and quietly exited. And I realized, having studied its species, that its violet dermis meant K had just said goodbye. I would never see K again.

Episode 6

Although K wouldn't take my calls after our last meeting, I got along well with the director of the Sevillian nanite lab who took it upon itself to give me a thorough overview of its craft while I waited for the foldship to make its scheduled return to Earth.

It turns out there are over a hundred types of nanite, including several which aren't intended to become part of a final structure. Orchestrating the dance of nanites to build a macroscopic structure, particularly a large one like a building, is a feat on the order of any kind of engineering humans have ever done. The one thing that is constant about nanites is their 400 micrometer edgewise cubical structure. It is that standard that makes the whole thing flow.

Along the way I took pictures of all the electron micrograph posters, and even went on a couple of field trips to see and take phone video of the construction process. A couple of days before departure I finally dared ask about the fold drive, and found my circumspection on the topic had been unnecessary. My host proudly told me there were four species of nanites that had no other purpose than to make critical parts of the fold generators, and while they knew the math and they knew the operating principle they didn't really have a way to make that kind of hardware without using the original nanites which had been given to them by the Curators.

Finally, over glasses of another stupidly expensive Earth brandy, I said I was curious about how the Curators intervene. The Sevillian I had fallen into the habit of calling L said that if I wanted to observe Curator activity, I really needed to find a world on the "critical path" between the introduction of agriculture and writing and the final maturation of space travel and the fold drive. "That is the interval when the Curators are most active in a species' development," it said. "It's a very clear thing from the archaeological record."

"Most active in *most* race's development," I kind of scowled.

"Ah, yes, our friend K told me. I have no explanation and hope you find one that is satisfactory." It turned out the Sevillians were aware of several such current critical path races, but there was no fold ship service to their worlds because the Curators enforced a quarantine.

Later, on Earth, the Director of our foldship project and several of his top aides listened intently to my account of all of this. They solemnly copied the photos off my phone and didn't even warn me about showing them around or talking about what had happened. "We really appreciate what you are doing," he said.

"I'm not sure what I *am* doing."

"I think you might be becoming our first ambassador to the galaxy."

Later, on what I thought at first was a random walk through the facility, we came to a large machine. "We are pretty sure this would solve our largest problem," he said. "It is a fold suppressor. The Universe doesn't actually like folds to come in contact, and it can be stopped. The math is sound and we're pretty sure it can't be overcome. The problem is it would also take us out of the interstellar community if we deployed it."

"Foldships could always slow down and come close by some other method."

"They really have no other method. Their foldships are so large they have no other practical drive than the fold generator itself, and if we disable that they would be helpless as they crashed in our gravity well. None of them would ever risk coming near such a thing."

"I might still feel safer with this thing running if our own people start making fold drives."

"Exactly, which is why we built and tested it. But we think something better is possible." We walked some more and came to a cavernous space being prepped for construction. "This is where we are going to build the fold span limiter."

I didn't want to sound stupid, so I just looked inquisitive.

The Director smiled. "The extent of the fold field in three-dimensional space is mostly determined by the mass surrounding the original fold point. It establishes a resonance in ten-dimensional space which fixes the size of the fold. Given a mostly solid spherical mass surrounding the fold point, the usual dimension is about three times the radius of the physical mass."

"So that's why if you fold off of the planet you take the whole planet with you?"

"It's a bit more complicated. If you don't know what you're doing you take the whole planet, but even if you know the constants and start at the surface, you take a chunk about the size of a large stadium."

"Still doesn't sound very practical."

"It's not. The thing is, the same principle that makes it possible to suppress the fold should also make it possible to limit the span of a fold. We are pretty sure we can make this thing and we are working on it 24/7. It would let us allow foldships to visit without allowing either our own crazies or anyone else to fold us off into the Sun. Basically it would only suppress folds that aren't properly configured."

"Sounds like a worthwhile project," I observed neutrally.

"Not our most important though," he said. We walked some more, finally through a garage door into the outdoors. We walked up to what I recognized as a two-seat trainer VTOL jump jet.

"Behold mankind's first starship," my host said."

"This thing has a fold drive? I thought the fold drive itself was bigger than this whole airplane."

"It is, if you make it with nanites. Our fabrication methods are flat but much finer. Our fold drive is about half a meter across. We chose this jet because its pressurization system wasn't hard to enhance for full vacuum. It can fall into the atmosphere and glide to the ground, then jump and fly high enough to safely fold out of the atmosphere with very little fuel."

"Have you ever flown it?"

"There's someone I want you to meet." I saw that a woman in uniform was walking toward us. He made introductions. "First human ambassador to the stars, meet our first starship pilot."

"I've taken it to every world in the Solar System," she said as we shook hands. "Let me tell you, Pluto is *weird*."

I looked at the Director. "Oh, we've recorded good scientific data, although we'll have to be careful releasing it," he said. "Within a few years everyone will know about this, but for now it's one of our biggest secrets."

"I'm not sure I am getting used to this," I said with a bit of a morbid chuckle.

"Oh, it's about to get a lot worse. Your next assignment is to go to one of the critical path worlds the Sevillians told you about and find evidence of Curator activity."

"Which one?"

"I figured I would leave that decision to you."

"I haven't been out of the Solar System yet," my pilot said reassuringly. "Looking forward to it."

So the very next day I was over a hundred light-years from Earth, this time in a craft made entirely by human industry, with a pilot who was having way too much fun as she folded us in and out of planetary gravity wells to check and match velocities. Finally we folded into the upper atmosphere of a world that looked a lot like Earth, Seville, or Pompeii.

"We'll be on the ground in about half an hour," M said from the front seat.

"We won't burn up?"

"We don't have orbital velocity. We'll fall until we can glide, then I'll start the engines to land us."

This all went according to plan until we landed in a clear area and popped the cockpit bubble. "Aren't we the first humans on this world?" I asked as M took off her pressure mask.

"Of course. The aliens don't come here, and this is the only human starship."

"Well then how is it that there's a human being standing at the edge of the clearing?"

He gave the appearance of a well-groomed British gentleman and he watched quietly as we stowed our gear and departed the starcraft. Once we were on the ground he approached and offered his hand, which we each shook cordially.

M deferred to me, as I was supposed to be the ambassador. "I thought we were the first humans here," I said with an attitude of respect and slight surprise.

"Oh, but you are," he said with a smile. "We perfected the art of walking among our children aeons ago. If I presented at any of your most advanced hospitals they would never suspect I am an alien, but I am in fact one of those you call Curators."

"We came here to find you," I said.

"I know. Earth is my normal assignment, obviously, but I was tasked to come here and intercept you when we realized you were going to break quarantine. Your cosmic acquaintances are both young species, like you barely out of quarantine themselves, and they did not understand and therefore communicate just how dangerous this is."

"Why?"

"We do not care much about what happens to species that have not reached the start of the critical path. They live and die all the time, accomplishing nothing, arousing no interest. And we consider it a duty of those species that have completed the critical path and gained space travel to learn to deal with the challenges they will find in the vastness of space and myriad interactions of interstellar commerce. Should you attempt a rampage of conquest they should be able to defend themselves.

"But the species on the critical path are interesting to us but vulnerable to premature influences and not yet able to defend themselves against invaders armed with high technology. We do not want you to recruit or prosyletize them or impose an order here. We want these beings to define their own order, refine it, reinforce it, then take it to the galaxy to participate in the vast garden that we have been creating for almost eight billion of your Earth years."

M spoke up. "You don't seem to have cared much for us on our critical path," she said with a sharp tone of bitterness.

"Your belligerence worried us," the Curator said unfazed. "You are far more willing to murder your brothers and sisters than is usual. We decided to develop you slowly so you might have time to mature beyond this impulse, but it happened that every time we thought it was a suitable time for a development, you had either done it already yourselves or were about to. In the latter cases we allowed you to advance on your own so you could own your achievement. For all your troubles your species has made remarkable accomplishments. Even though you made it from a murder weapon your craft here is a wonderfully and uniquely small and maneuverable starship."

"It didn't occur to you to intervene to help us with our belligerence, rather than leave us to our own devices?"

He shrugged. "It was a judgement call. Your rate of advancement has been startling. We underestimated the effect the threat of mutual murder would have even on those of you not inclined so much to fratricide, since you had to defend yourselves against the dangerous minority. Of course your dangerous ones tend to find high office in your political systems, which is an ongoing problem. For aeons our policy has been one of mostly nonintervention. Sometimes our children kill themselves instead of developing; it's a natural part of what we are trying to encourage. We have had other murderous children, but none so technologically successful as yourselves."

"And now we have the fold drive."

"Yes. It will be interesting to see what you do with it. It is as dangerous as it is useful. Only a handful of species in all of our experience have ever gone to the trouble to build nuclear weapons. The ability to make a big messy poisonous explosion is rather unimpressive next to what a fold drive can do, and most of our children get the fold drive without ever building the massive industrial works you have made."

"And with nanites, any individual person who wants to can make a fold drive."

"Exactly."

"So what happens next?"

"You leave this world and don't come back to any critical path quarantine world. We mostly consider you your own and our childrens' problem, but we will not tolerate interference in our gardening. The Sevillians misled you on one point because they don't know the truth themselves. Our standards are reasonable and none of our children have been stupid enough to fold their homeworld into its star by accident once we gave them the proper configuration parameters. But a few worlds have been folded into their stars. We do not seek to create an ordered formal garden; we want to be surprised by our children. Nothing would be more boring and pointless to us than a galaxy full of life that we designed, performing to some perfect specification. But even so once in awhile we do have to weed."

"Is that a threat?" M asked sharply.

"Just a warning. Our requirements are few and reasonable. I will give you half an hour to depart. If you do not you will never see Earth again." And he disappeared into thin air.

"What the hell!" M rushed forward and pawed the ground where he had been standing.

"Tell me he didn't fold out from the surface of a planet."

"He folded out. He didn't take any of the vegetation or leave anything of himself. There was no air pressure pop. *How the hell did he do that?*"

"Come on, we have to leave."

"We have to find out how he did that!"

"And we never will if he folds us off to the other side of the galaxy, which I think is what he was implying if we don't leave. He just showed us something extremely valuable."

"And what's that? We are nowhere near being able to do anything like this."

"No, but now that we know it's possible, we can start trying to figure out how he did it."

Episode 7

As I climbed down from the thing that had once been just an airplane, it hit me hard that this was a starship, a human-built and human-owned starship, and we had just taken it to a world circling another star without any help from anybody. They hadn't put a lot of effort into cosmetic customization and it was still the same drab semi-camo olive green they love for subsonic warplanes that don't have the sexy new stealth stuff going for them. I realized the foldship project had probably rescued it from a scrap pile.

"Does this thing have a name?" I asked M as she secured her gear.

"We call it the test article," she said with a shrug. "It's the only one of its kind we have."

"Well it won't be for long. Do you think it's a good idea for the history books to say we just took humanity's first self propelled trip to another star in the 'test article?'"

She looked at the craft thoughtfully. "Well I hear *you're* the namer of alien worlds. What would you call it?"

"I'd favor Firefly, except that's kind of used... wait, it's green and we went from the ground here to the ground there. How about Grasshopper?"

She looked at the craft thoughtfully then motioned for me to follow. We winded among aircraft, mostly in various states of disassembly, until we got to a mechanics' area. "Are the paint guys here?" M asked loudly.

"Yeah, we're here."

"Can I get the name Grasshopper painted on the fold project test article?"

"By whose authority?"

"I'm the aircraft's commander."

Once the higher-ups realized what had happened M and I were separated for debriefing. Since we hadn't thought to record it they went over our conversation with the Curator until everyone was sure we had it right syllable for syllable, and different sketch artists worked from our descriptions. Finally we were reunited in a conference room where we faced about thirty people, mostly scientists and engineers with military backgrounds, before the Director.

"This is not a tribunal or anything like that," the Director told us. "We just need to figure out where we stand, and you're at the focal point right now."

M and I both nodded.

"How serious is the threat these Curators pose?"

M gave me an "I'm just the pilot" look. Of course in addition to being a test pilot she was a graduate level physicist and part of the team that had built the fold drive, but of the two of us I was apparently the diplomat.

"If we piss them off enough it's existential," I said, "but I think he wanted to make it clear that it would also be hard to piss them off that much and fairly easy to keep them uninterested in us. Going to a quarantined critical path world is one of the *few* things they really care about."

"And what was the nature of the threat he made if you would have stayed?"

I looked at M. "He threatened to fold us off to the other side of the galaxy. We would have had no way to navigate home or even to find nearby habitable worlds. It would have been a death sentence."

"But not a threat to Earth. Not to fold us into the Sun."

"Not in that case. But he did make it clear that it had gone that far before with a few other species. Sometimes they do have to weed their galactic garden."

The voices changed but the tone didn't really. These were mostly military personnel and they didn't like the idea of limits being placed on them. "What does it take to piss them off that much?"

"I'm not sure I want to know," I said. "Do we really need to push them?"

The Director spoke up. "In all our talks with aliens, none have ever mentioned a conversation like this with a Curator. They get gifts, but never interaction. Not even the most distant stories or legends of such an encounter. No hint that they know or even think that the Curators walk among them in disguise. We'll have to follow this up but I have to think this was a pretty extraordinary intervention on their part."

"He called the ship 'wonderful' and 'unique,'" M said. "I had the impression he was using our language very precisely—J?"

"I agree," I said. "Those were the only superlatives he used except for the ones describing our fetish for murder."

"The test article is just a tiny test ship not even capable of docking with another vessel or carrying passengers in proper spacesuits," someone in the audience said. "It doesn't even make a proper substitute for our rocket shuttles to their fold ships. What could possibly make it so extraordinary?"

M seemed to be looking into some far place. "It's a grasshopper," she said.

"What?"

"J did his naming thing again," the Director said. "The test article is being named Grasshopper for whatever reason. M is its commander so it's her right and decision."

"We departed the surface of a planet, folded, and landed on the surface of another planet. They can't do that. *None* of them can do that. Isn't that right, J?"

M had never met an alien other than the Curator, but I had spent hundreds of hours talking to them. "I think you might be right."

"It's a self contained ship that can leave from the surface of a world, fold to another, and land on its surface. All their foldships require ground support to do transport from ground to orbit. We don't even *need* to orbit because we can just drop into the atmosphere and land on the damn surface." Her eyes got wider. "And the Curators do it their own way, with the even higher technology. We crossed a barrier they set for their children, in a way they didn't expect." She took a sip of water. "They've been doing this curation thing for eight billion years and they've never seen it before," she said in a tone of awe.

"That seems like..."

"...exactly what happened," I said. "I was there, and she's right. The Curator was impressed, and he was establishing position." I took a sip of water. "He made a point of mentioning that he could pass for human even in a hospital. I think he meant that for me, since I'm a doctor. He *knew* I was a doctor. He wanted to remind me that they have a very fine degree of control over biology. As if the so-called mark of the Curators hadn't suggested that. Forgive me rocket scientists, but I think getting to the stage of disguising yourself as an alien life form effectively enough to present at an alien hospital is probably a bit harder than even making a fold drive."

"Could your visitor have simply been human?"

"If so, one well equipped with alien technology, well versed in their technology and culture, and ready to go to action in a matter of days. As M mentioned the precision of his language, I also tend to think he wouldn't do prevarication. The Curators operate from a point from which such unpleasantness just isn't necessary. When you really have the power you don't have to misrepresent what you can do."

"We need to carefully explore our options," the Director said. "While I'm currently more worried by what our own idiots would do with a fold drive, we may have made a faux pas here. What are the permitted parameters? We don't need *another* threat from godlike aliens."

"If I may offer a suggestion," a very old gentleman said from the back of the room. Unlike most of the participants he wasn't wearing a uniform. "As I understand, we have visited two types of alien world, a few civilized worlds with space travel and now a 'critical path' world with a species transitioning from agriculture to space travel. Did the alien not say they didn't care about worlds that hadn't reached the critical path?"

"That is exactly what he said," M and I said more or less simultaneously.

"So we humans completed the critical path much faster than normal, but it normally takes at most a hundred thousand or maybe even a million years. And of course those worlds which have completed the critical path are potential enemies if we try to invade them. But the Earth was habitable for beings such as ourselves for most of half a billion years before we finally emerged to start on our own critical path. The Curators have been making worlds like the Earth all over the galaxy for aeons. It seems that many, maybe even most, of those worlds in the habitable zone with properly placed moons and water and introduced life must be somewhere between our Cambrian Explosion and the rise of our own agricultural ancestors."

"So?"

"If I am reading this transcript right, I think we were just offered those worlds if we want them."

M and I looked at one another, and our eyes widened in recognition. The Curator had told us the worlds we weren't allowed to go to and the worlds he expected to challenge us if we threatened them. He hadn't mentioned that there were a lot of others nobody cared about waiting to be explored or even colonized. The negative space in his warning was our gift.

"Why wouldn't the other aliens have gone to these worlds?" another voice asked.

M seemed to grow about half a meter and said "Because they can't get to the ground! The aliens' fold drives are big and their fold ships are too big to land so they need to orbit, and they need ground based support to travel from orbit to the surface. But *we* have a ship that can simply go to the ground and get back up without ground support on any world with an oxygen atmosphere."

"Which," I said, "thanks to the Curators, should be a lot of them."

It was suddenly obvious why the Curator had called the Grasshopper "wonderful."

"May I ask who you are?" M asked of the man who had made this suggestion.

"Oh, I just wrote a couple of science fiction stories. But these guys liked them."

"Why can't the aliens make a craft like our ... Grasshopper?"

Another authoritative voice. "They make everything of nanites, so their methods are coarse. Nanites are seductively convenient but once they bond themselves in place to make a larger thing, a lot of the underlying structure is still there for now mission-useless things like moving around and energy conversion and following the assembly plan. The coarseness limits the resolution of their fold operations. The smallest fold drive they can make is bigger than the entire Grasshopper, and far too heavy to make a winged much less VTOL surface landing."

"What about the alien folding off the world directly?"

"If they made that fold drive by true nanoassembly, an atom at a time, that kind of precision should be possible in a device you could put in your pocket," another voice said. "We've been arguing in our group about whether that could ever be possible. I think our astronauts have given us a direction for research."

I felt a bit of a swell at that. I wasn't just a dermatologist, even a world-famous one with celebrity clients. I was an *astronaut*.

"Is that kind of assembly even possible?" someone asked.

"The nanites do it themselves in the process of reproduction. They nanodisassemble one of their own kind and execute a gang copy operation simultaneously making millions of atom by atom copies. This process is also how they copy things like small amounts of frozen food and drink. But the nanites cannot create new designs, only copy what already exists, and in very small chunks. To make a pocket fold drive you'd have to make an original design the size of, say, a balled fist all in one go. That involves a hell of a lot of atomic placements."

"It must be possible though, if our witnesses are accurate."

"There is another thing," someone else said. "The ability to make a fold drive implies the ability to detect fold operations at a distance. This is how the Sevillians found us. But all during our research we have detected occasional hints of fold activity at close range and small scale. We have observed such events on almost a daily basis. We had written them off as noise or interference, but this suggests the possibility that we are detecting Curator activity."

The room erupted in a chorus of exclamations. The Director had to pound his folding table to restore order.

"Wouldn't the aliens have detected these activities?"

"They build their fold drives in orbit, and their resolution is low. For their equipment it probably would be below the true noise threshold."

"I think we have several courses for new action," the Director almost shouted. "The fold drive team needs to look into these possible Curator fold events. The nanite team needs to look into nanoassembly at larger scale, and liaise with the fold team about what they might need you to be able to do to move forward. We have completed and are testing another actual fold drive assembly, with a third nearing completion, and we need to be considering what kind of craft to make with them. And our pilot and ambassador need to find us worlds we can safely explore and colonize."

"How will we find them?" M asked.

"I have a surprise of my own. At about the time you were leaving the critical path world, we received a gift from the Curators. Apparently our first in a long time." He showed us a keychain memory unit. "It was encrypted with our best algorithm, using our own administrative password, and placed on one of our most secure servers in a place where we couldn't fail to notice it. Our network guys were quite impressed, but if the Curators can really pass as human and fold past our security systems it might not imply that great of a computer hacking ability. Anyway it is a digital map of the galaxy. The instructions are in Esperanto and very clear. It lists every quarantined world and every developed world in the galaxy. I checked, and Earth is there. We are listed as developed and spacefaring, just like Seville and Pompeii."

"How does that help us find undeveloped worlds?" someone asked.

"The Curators have been curating worlds for aeons. Given the incubation time there should be plenty that aren't listed. If we find a world that's habitable and not on this list, it should be open."

Finding Earthlike worlds is hard at interstellar distances but not so hard when you can visit a star and flit about it with the fold drive. Within three weeks we had an instrumentation package for the Grasshopper that made it possible to map all the worlds of a candidate solar system within an hour or two by doing a dozen sky scans from the vertices of an imaginary icosahedron around the star. After that our main immediate limitation was that we had only one craft to do both the sky surveys and ground investigations. Even so, within a month M and I had found and walked on half a dozen Earthlike worlds, and nobody had challenged us about our presence on any of them.

Episode 8

I had never been much of a camper, but M had to take a geologist on a mission to another world and our newest starship was scheduled to arrive within a day. I awoke to the droning of the C130's jet engines. I kicked the switch that turned on the battery powered LED landing lights and got out of the tent in time to see a row of parachutes blossom in the morning sky.

The Boxcar couldn't land yet, having no landing strip, but that was also the purpose of this mission. As it popped off into the first fold back home, the last of the parachutes to emerge from the plane turned out to be lighter and more maneuverable than those floating pallets of tools and materials to the surface. One of those landed near me and the serviceman saluted me as he advanced. "Sir, are you Ambassador J?" he asked earnestly.

"Son, we are eighty light-years from the Earth, and my pilot is both female and on another mission, so that's kind of an obvious thing," I said dryly.

A few minutes later his commanding officer got to me. "Ambassador," he said simply with an outstretched hand, which I shook vigorously.

"We are going to build you the finest damn airstrip this planet has ever seen," he said with a sharklike grin.

THE CURATORS

"I appreciate that, but I hope you realize that's kind of a low bar to clear." We both laughed and he turned around. "Men, let's get the quarters raised. The Ambassador is probably tired of sleeping on the ground and eating MRE's."

Within a couple of hours they had a large tent erected, and were populating it with folding beds and tables. These were Seabees, the Navy's Construction Battalion, and they were doing what they had done on every corner of the Earth for nearly a hundred years.

A few hours later I was being asked to address the men. "Ambassador J, have you chosen a name for this place?" the Admiral asked.

"I have," I said. "Welcome to the world of Providence."

There was applause. "So are we under the protection of God as we do our work here?" he asked a little later.

"That's not actually why I chose the name," I said, but I didn't explain it just then.

The men fanned out. There were both a small river and a limestone formation nearby, which were the main reasons our geologist chose this location for our first off-Earth project. The Seabees had brought everything else necessary to make a concrete airstrip. The process was scheduled to take about two weeks.

"Boxcar seems like a rather prosaic name for our second starship," the Admiral said as we were dishing out a welcome meal of fried chicken and mashed potatoes.

"Does it now," I said. "You know there was once a guy named Fred Bock who was commander of a B-29 in World War Two. His craft was named Bock's Car and that was what was painted on its nose. And while Bock didn't pilot the mission, that was the plane that Charles Sweeney commanded to drop our second atomic bomb, Fat Man, on the city of Nagasaki. And let's face it, it's a cargo craft, so it basically is an airborne boxcar."

The next day I heard a familiar engine scream and Grasshopper landed near to our original small tent. I introduced M and her geologist to the Seabees, and we had turkey and dressing for dinner.

The Boxcar returned about three times a day to drop more supplies by parachute. Eventually the airstrip began to emerge, starting as a rough area graded by a couple of small all-terrain machines. Within a week the concrete plant was making Portland cement, the grinder was making and sorting aggregate, and the batcher was mixing it all with water from the nearby stream to make concrete.

M had to go home for a report and offered to take me with her, but I wanted to see the airstrip construction through to completion. As it turned out she was back before the airstrip was done. But it was well on its way, a flat strip of hard surface that would be over three thousand meters long when it was ready. The Boxcar kept returning and dropping parachutes and generators, lighting, and painting supplies were added to our kit.

There was also wine and whiskey, and after a few days the Admiral asked me over dinner the inevitable question. "Why Providence?"

"Well it's the capital of Rhode Island," I said.

"And of the fifty states, you chose to honor Rhode Island by naming our first interstellar colony after its capital?"

THE CURATORS

"Providence was founded by Roger Williams after he got kicked out of Massachusetts," I said. "It was the first place where actual religious freedom was practiced in the New World. Before Williams, all the colonies were founded as theocracies."

"That's pretty good. Williams must have been one forward looking person."

I actually snorted my bourbon. "Oh, on the contrary," I said laughing out loud. "Roger Williams was one of the most horribly stubborn fundamentalists ever to live. He believed literally that only 144,000 people could ever get into Heaven. He was kicked out of Massachusetts because the other Puritans considered him too extreme."

Several seconds of awkward silence. Then the Admiral asked, "Well then why did you name this world for his capital?"

"He reasoned that if God had placed his chosen few in the midst of so many of the damned, that it must mean that God must have meant for the chosen to find a way to live in peace among the damned. It meant that even the natives and other heathens should be taken seriously. Williams is the reason religious freedom was written into the Constitution of the United States. Not because he believed all religion was valid, but because he believed it was his duty to live in peace among those damned to Hell."

As I finished saying that I saw glasses being lifted into the air. "To Providence then," a lot of men said in unison, and I raised my glass to join them.

The next day Boxcar finally landed on the world of Providence, and was followed shortly by the City of New Orleans, another starship that had once been a C130 but unlike the Boxcar was fitted for passenger rather than cargo service.

One of the men who got off the New Orleans was an Army General. "You need to keep thinking of names," he said with a chuckle. "We're looking to buy a few surplus Boeing 747's."

"I thought those had mostly been retired from service," I said.

"Oh, they have. But the use case for them as long distance aircraft on Earth isn't nearly as good as that for them as fold drive starships."

Later that evening I wandered out onto the airstrip and realized that it was really a lot larger then necessary for a C130. The military guys were thinking ahead of the game and out of the box. This first airstrip humans ever built on another world was one that could readily accommodate a Boeing 747.

Episode 9

One Year Later

The starship Olympic departed from the passenger terminal at JFK like any other aircraft. As a VIP I made my way to the upstairs lounge and was issued a pair of Velcro slippers. After the converted 747 took off it climbed out over the Atlantic Ocean and at 3000 meters began a series of fold transfers designed to minimize the amount of air we were taking with us into outer space. After about ten of these we were 100 kilometers up, and folded out to Neptune to spend three hours falling into its gravity well. Flight attendants took over, passing out alcoholic drinks in squeeze bulbs and Velcro slippers to those passengers who needed to visit the rest rooms. The Captain came on and announced how to view Neptune's moons Triton and Nereid and some surface storms that were visible.

We now had over thirty runways and a half-dozen serviceable airports on more than a dozen extrasolar worlds, and we were just starting our galactic exploration. The new world of Pretoria had only had its airstrip for a couple of months and was still very undeveloped, although some special projects were under way that were considered a bit dangerous for a more populated world. M was waiting for me at the edge of the tarmac, and soon I had packed my little camping bag in Dragonfly and we were off to an even newer and more distant world.

We spent several days scouting sites for cities and airports and doing a little more than just camping together. It was all peaceful R&R until M woke me up in the middle of the night. "J, you need to go to the Grasshopper right now. Don't gather anything or hesitate. We have to get out of here."

I had seen M in her role as a military officer a few times and I knew better than to argue. We had parked Grasshopper far enough away to avoid knocking our tent down as it took off or landed. I was climbing into the rear seat when there was a bright flash of light and I looked back to see our tent engulfed by a fireball.

"What the..."

"Quickly!" She was already in her seat, coping secured, and starting the engines. As Grasshopper rose into the air another bomb went off between the tent and our takeoff point.

"Okay, why am I in the jump seat in my pajamas?"

"Because you don't prefer to sleep naked. Also, Grasshopper monitors continuously for fold events now. I had some alarms set. We've never known quite what to look for but there are a few things that we knew wouldn't be normal. There's a foldship overhead and it's not in orbit. It's positioned right over us to act as a bomber."

"Did we know the aliens could do that?"

"We knew it was within the range of their demonstrated tech. We gamed out how it might work if we wanted to use their tech as a weapon. We didn't know if any of them had gone to the same trouble. These guys can obviously aim."

"Well they missed the ship."

THE CURATORS

"J, I'm pretty sure they want to *steal* the ship. Wouldn't do them much good if they bombed it." She punched the fold drive and folded us straight out of the atmosphere, to a point a few hundred miles away. Within a few seconds the giant foldship appeared distressingly close. M folded again, and the alien ship followed appearing even closer.

"Well, they can track fold events. No big surprise there."

"What if you fold out further?"

"I don't want to get too far from the planet. If they try any kind of energy or projectile weapon on us, we might have to make an unpowered re-entry."

"They're coming closer."

M used the RCS jets to nudge us away, but the foldship came after us. It wasn't as maneuverable as we were but it had a lot more power at its disposal. Grasshopper's air breathing engines don't function in vacuum so in space it depends on the relatively small RCS rockets and batteries.

"Well this is something I never expected to need so soon. You might want to close your eyes, J."

"Why?"

"You don't have a welder's mask back there, and you don't want to be blinded." I closed my eyes and despite that my vision was blasted with white light. I threw an arm up to block it and it barely helped. The light was hot and searing and ended as quickly as it had begun. When I was able to open my eyes the alien ship was quite a bit further away, and there was a giant hole in its side.

"*What* in the name of the Curators was *that*?"

"Well, you know those nifty little communicators they use so their not so smart tablets can phone home? They call them microfold generators. They're not capable of passing matter, only massless particles like photons, and only across a relatively limited transfer aperture. There's a project going on Pretoria to open one of those into the photosphere of the Sun and use the solar energy to fire a steam electric generating plant. Much more energy dense than the aliens' methods and we have all the other tech developed. Well, along come my people with their Mars hats on, and... wait a minute. Fuck, they're not in orbit."

"So?"

"They're falling to the surface. They can't stop it. The suicidal idiots didn't give themselves orbital velocity and now if they can't fold out they're all going to die."

"My heart bleeds for them. Didn't they just try to kill us?"

"Yes, and...this is weird. Their fold drive still seems to still have some functionality, but it looks like OH MY GOD!"

She punched us out to well beyond the world's Moon, just in time to watch the entire planet disappear in a brief explosion of sunlight.

Episode 10

M took us back to Pretoria, since that's where the Grasshopper was expected. Fortunately M's landing spot and quonset hut were fairly remote from the airstrip's active area because I had to loan her my pajama top for us to get to her quarters. M doesn't like to wear bedclothes.

"What I don't understand," she said as we were getting dressed, "is if they meant to steal Grasshopper, how they expected to get it back to their foldship. It's the main reason we've gone unchallenged on all these worlds; with their nanite tech the aliens could get down with a little imagination, but getting back up from the surface without infrastructure is their big problem."

"Perhaps I can help with that," a familiar voice said. He just appeared in the room, like a ghost materializing where neither of us happened to be looking. "I realize you want to report to your people, but at the moment I think it's rather more important for you to let us know what happened."

The Curator listened carefully as we related our story. When we were done, he said "I am afraid we bear some fault for this. We knew you were doing new things but we failed to warn you of some of the hazards you might encounter. We really didn't expect for you to encounter raiders so soon, as their homeworld and usual operating theatre is half-way around the Wheel of the Galaxy. But the news of your activities has traveled far, and they apparently decided your tech would be of benefit to them."

"Raiders?"

"Not such a young species, but much like yourselves, belligerent and capable of great selfishness. The act of folding out the entire world when they realized they were doomed is typical. We mourn the loss of so much of our effort, particularly knowing you were thinking of making use of the place."

"But you say they're like us. Aren't we also a threat?"

"It is a matter of debate among us, but at the moment we favor waiting and seeing. So far your kind are making your destiny, not stealing it from others. I was greatly relieved that it wasn't your fold drive that annihilated the planet."

"We've worked hard to make sure our drives can't be detuned that way. A few of our early ones still can, but we are scheduled to destroy them and replace them with more secure ones in the near future."

"See, that is a clear difference between yourselves and the raiders. They really do not see how the threat they pose looks to other species. You have individuals with that problem but you also know that that is a problem. The raiders unfortunately have a thoroughgoing culture teaching that strength and victory are the only virtues."

"Great, space Vikings."

"They also resemble your fictional Star Trek Klingons."

"You mentioned earlier you had some idea how they planned to get Grasshopper up to their ship."

THE CURATORS

"Yes. You noticed they don't believe in making orbit on a raid. If they can conduct a raid in a few minutes, they can do it in the time their ship takes to fall only a short distance toward the surface. And matching surface velocity instead of making orbit makes their operations fast. It's much easier to get something to space than to orbit, as your species has learned to great precision, and the raiders have guided solid-fuel rockets capable of doing that job for modest payloads. And strategically, it gives them an advantage because if their ship is over a city, you don't dare disable it even if you could. Had their raid gone as planned, after killing you they would have strapped solid fuel boosters to the Grasshopper and flown it out of the atmosphere, where their fold ship could engulf it at low relative velocity before folding off."

"We have to get serous about building defenses," M said.

"We have to worry a bit about our other children."

"The raiders aren't coming for your other children," M said decisively. "We have something they want and they know it. And now we have to make sure they don't ever get it."

"You have spread yourselves a bit thin," the Curator warned.

"Only because we didn't know. We have ten billion people. We have over a hundred mothballed 747's waiting to be turned into starships, and we're making a fold drive every month now. Tell me something, how many fold ships does the typical spacefaring species maintain?"

"Three would be considered an extravagant fleet. They are like your naval aircraft carriers self-contained worlds. Before this incident we believe the raiders had eight."

"I don't think we're going to be doing it that way. If you don't mind, I think I need to get to Earth and talk to some people about this."

"By all means." M stormed out, and minutes later I heard Grasshopper firing up. "Ambassador, how do you feel about all this?"

"The raiders are murderous," I said. "We used to be, and some of our individuals still are, but people like M are going to try to harness this power without giving it to the barbarians to use to burn the galaxy down."

"We will give you your chance then," he said. "Just be aware that there is a certain point at which we will have no choice but to intervene, even if it means burning all of *your* works down."

I just nodded and he disappeared.

Episode 11

I returned to Earth commercially, again on the converted 747 Olympic. I wondered as I boarded how many of those original Boeing engineers were still around, and how it would feel for them to know that their 1960's era aircraft had been saved from the scrapheap by their usefulness as starships.

On the flight home—well, it's not really a "flight," it's more a "fall" into Neptune's gravity well to adjust our velocity to match that of Earth—I used sticky pads to organize some of the documents M and I had assembled about our still unnamed new world. Some of those related to files on my tablet computer and I spent some time watching them. Everything we had gone to the trouble to record—the pond where we had had a romantic frolic, the beaches where we had run, the dramatic mesa where we had envisioned high altitude runways, and of course every living thing—all of it was gone in a fraction of a second. Part of me wanted to delete the files and burn the documents, but another part of me realized these were now the only records left of this world, a world as vibrant and habitable as Earth had been just a hundred thousand years ago before humans entered the critical path, that would now ever exist.

I did not realize I was quietly sobbing until a man in uniform pushed a drink on me. "I know," he said. "I trained M at

Edwards. You aren't a warrior, J. This is an awful thing for you to have to bear."

I tasted the squeeze bulb. It was good old uncut Jack D. "Not sure how this fixes anything," I sniffled.

"Some things you can't fix," the General said. "All you can do is leave them as best as you can manage. You're a good man, a better man for this than most of my colleagues." I finally looked across and realized that I was talking to a senior Cabinet member. I had never met anyone within three pay grades of him despite what I had been doing with the aliens.

"I don't know what to do with this stuff," I said, unable to think of anything else.

"Well, preserve it of course. Given your brief time there it will make a rather small and obviously inadequate museum, but in my line of work we consider memory important. When you are trained to kill things, you have to understand them to be able to kill them. And sometimes when you come to understand a thing, you realize that killing it is not the correct solution. And sometimes you realize the wrong thing happened, and you need to be reminded and your students taught how it happened so we can avoid doing it again."

I composed myself a bit and nodded. I realized that he had used the word "students" with some deliberation. I did not consider myself a teacher but entire worlds of people would study and judge what I was doing. Then the Captain announced that we were about to fold Earthward and gravity would become a bit unpredictable as we fell into the thin upper atmosphere, so we should all strap in.

Back on Earth I saw that of a line of six 747's lined up at jetways, four were starships. Humans were doing amazing things. But at what risk?

I soon got another shock. The man who had comforted me on the ship had actually been sent to retrieve me. The Sevillian fold ship had returned early, and their ambassador was demanding to meet with me—not anyone else.

We only had one 747 fold shuttle, the specially modified Crossbridge, which could dock with the Sevillians. We had obviously stopped using chemical rockets once we got the fold drives working reliably on converted aircraft. Crossbridge was an awkward craft with a big telescoping tube sticking out of its rear to meet the docking ring, and an extra-large RCS system. We were working on other solutions but it had been a bit of a quick hack.

"K," I said in astonishment as the airlock opened.

"I wish I could say it gives me pleasure to see you again," K said. "But I'm afraid it is the opposite."

"I know, we have a situation..."

"I have prevailed on our council to halt our excursions to your world. We will no longer visit Earth. I wanted to tell you this directly."

"Why?"

"J, your kind have destroyed a fold ship and a *world*. I hope you are proud of yourselves."

"That's not exactly fair. We were attacked, and we didn't fold the planet off. We've been making sure our fold drives can't do that."

"Yours aren't the only fold drives though. Ours, the only ones we have ever known, cannot be locked down as you suggest. You have attracted raiders to our part of the galaxy. You have created new weapons. Before you arrived the raiders were a contained threat. Now, if they get your fold drive, they could be far more dangerous. And that's not even to consider your foldship destroying 'sunlight cannon.' Made from our *communicator* technology! We do not need this excrement in our domicile."

"I'm sorry you feel that way, but..."

"You have destroyed an equilibrium which has been stable for more than a billion of your years, that was in place before the Curators told your single-celled ancestors how to assemble themselves into multicellular structures. I just wish we could go back in time and let you destroy yourselves instead of helping you."

"We weren't going to destroy ourselves, K. Even the small danger of folding our dead world Mars into the Sun was past by the time you noticed us."

"We'll just see how that works out for you then. From a distance." And my old friend K, to whom I had once bared my entire body so it could confirm there was no Mark of the Curators, turned on its awkward-looking insectoid heels and stalked off.

For the next two days I busied myself organizing our records of the destroyed world. I wasn't sure where the museum would be or how it would be accessed but the General had asked me to preserve them, so I preserved them.

Finally M returned from her debriefing with the foldship project people. "We have to get over this," she said when she saw how upset I was.

THE CURATORS

"I just saw a planet destroyed," I snapped. "How do I get over that?"

"It might not hurt that our guys have the fold span limiter working."

"So Earth is safe?"

"Our personal Curator even stopped by to assure me that it is an elegant solution that fortunately doesn't limit their activities. They would have been a bit upset if we had deployed the fold inhibitor instead."

"Would it have inhibited their really advanced fold fields?"

"A fold is a fold, and if you can't make it it doesn't matter what the target aperture is. He was very polite about it but hinted that they would have had no choice but to destroy a functioning inhibitor. I also got the strong impression that nobody, including the Curators themselves, had ever considered trying to build a span limiter, probably because they were depending on self-interest and the lack of remote control to discourage anyone from turning a fold drive into a weapon that way. And also possibly because making a span limiter out of nanites is either unworkable or impossible."

"They can fold themselves off from the surface of a planet without disturbing the air or the grass they're standing on but we made better technology than theirs?"

"It's different. Just as our air breathing jet starships are different from anything else any of them have done in billions of years because none of them have ever had a good reason to build a jet engine, and you can't build one with nanites."

The General on the Olympic had left me the last half of the bottle of Jack Daniel's and I poured myself another glass. "This is some crazy shit and I'm not sure I know how to to deal with it," I said to the wall with my back turned to her.

"J," she said softly, touching my shoulder. "I was trained to kill people by pushing a button from five klicks up. Nobody ever trained you that way. You just wanted people to feel better about themselves by giving them clearer skin." And she hugged me and made a sound that as half laugh and half sob.

"How we will ever get through this?" I asked her.

"Let's start by having some pancakes."

Episode 12

I busied myself working with M and her colleagues on a number of working groups, trying to figure out how to best defend Earth and our new colonies and to deal with our suddenly dubious position within the galactic culture. Then one night I woke up stone cold alert straight out of a dream as if I'd been ejected from it, and woke M up by shouting, "I KNOW HOW TO FIX THIS!"

M stirred in her sleep and said "fix it in the morning."

In the morning I went to the facility commander and told him I wanted to make a proposal to everyone at once. I had been something of a hotshot alien specialist before being attacked by aliens myself, so this was given some priority. After another week we filled a conference room with scientists, engineers, military brass, and a couple of politicians. I had told them only that I had a possible comprehensive solution to our raider problem, and I wanted to present it all at once so it could be digested, challenged, and defended all at once.

"We have big problems," I opened. "We know we can kill a raider ship and prevent it from folding our world into the Sun, but we also know they like to park their fold ships stationary with respect to the ground, so that they fall if they can't fold out, and a three mile wide fold ship is a hell of a falling object.

It's not fair but the Sevillians have ostracized us and there is a limit to what we can ask of the Pompeiians, much less the other races we have even less contact with. And we all know how much help we've gotten from the Curators."

I paused for a moment. "I have a simple proposal. I know it will sound strange but I ask you to hear me out. I propose that we find the raiders and *give* them everything they tried to steal, and at least one more thing beyond that."

To call what happened next in that room "pandemonium" would be to do it a disservice. In the front row M regarded me with eyes widened by shock, and the Cabinet member who had come to Pretoria to fetch me regarded me with strange calm. He eventually got up, joined me onstage, pulled a service pistol and fired it into the ceiling. I was thinking it must be loaded with blanks when I felt bits of plaster falling on my head.

"Shut the fuck up and let's hear him out," he said. Then he turned to me and said, "This better be good, son."

"First," I said, "We need to talk about Vikings." And I talked about Vikings, and many other things, and there were protests and challenges and counterarguments and after four hours a speaker phone call to the White House. And after that the decision was made to follow my recommendation.

I was pleasantly surprised to find the door to M's dorm unlocked. She had even gotten a fresh bottle of bourbon. Moving in silence she made me a drink and handed it to me.

"I hope you aren't..."

"Part of me wants to kill you," she said in a tone that made it very clear she would be quite capable of doing that if sufficiently inspired. She poured herself a drink.

"And the other part of you?"

She knocked the entire drink back. I had the sense she had done that a few times before I arrived. "That part knows you're right. God help us."

"Did someone call for help?" a familiar voice asked.

"I thought you hardly ever communicated directly with your children," M said.

"You have proven more extraordinary than most. I would not have missed that presentation for anything. Very surprising, of course. Not at all what any of us expected."

"And what would you think of your troublesome raider children spreading out through the galaxy?"

"As with yourselves, as long as they do not molest the critical path worlds we don't care. Developed worlds have everything the raiders do, and as for the others our mandate is carbon based intelligent life on as many worlds as possible. You and the raiders are both carbon based intelligent life forms."

"And how many worlds get destroyed in the process?"

"It has been over a billion years since a world was folded into its star," the Curator said. "We live much longer than you, but we are not immortal, so you two are the only living beings in the entire galaxy who have ever actually seen it happen in person." He bowed his head. "And it was my people who did it the last time, for reasons I'd rather not discuss."

"Wow," M and I said more or less at the same time.

"Anyway, you spent some time discussing the first quest of your proposal, finding the Raiders, since they are on the other side of the galaxy and didn't leave a calling card." He extended his hand and offered me a folded Post-It note. When I opened it I saw a hand written seven digit number.

"We recently gave you a map of the galaxy," he said. "Every developed world is listed. The list is indexed. That number is the index of the raiders' world." And poof, he disappeared.

This new gift turned what had seemed like a long term project into a much shorter term one. After much discussion everyone agreed that there was only one team to send on the first mission, and we decided to use the original C130 Boxcar rather than one of our newer and more capable ships. We did upgrade its fold drive, and install better fuel cells for out of atmosphere power.

The engineers had a bit of work to do on one part of my proposal, particularly working out how to adapt some of it to a nanite-based technology. But as I had guessed, it was a reasonable challenge.

Being on the other side of the galaxy, the raider world was moving at about 400 kilometers per second relative to Sol and the Earth, and it took ten hours of falling toward Neptune with twelve folds to rough out the difference. Before we folded across the galaxy we were going fast enough to go from the Earth to the Moon in about an hour.

And then we didn't fold out to the exact coordinates. Our instruments aren't calibrated to that kind of precision, and we had never folded such a distance before. M was learning as much as she was practicing skill as she figured out where we were based on the known points on the galaxy map and sharpened our position toward the raider homeworld. Finding the world itself, the other worlds of its system, a suitable gas world to use as a thrust attractor, and actually matching velocity took two more days.

THE CURATORS

The raiders could of course detect fold activity, and when we made low orbit they were waiting for us. "You've never done this before, have you?" was our greeting.

"Not from such a distance," M said. "We seek the beings known as raiders. We bring gifts."

"We are the raiders, but others would warn that buying us off doesn't work."

"We do not bring Danegeld." I was pretty sure that translated as *screee* on the other end. "We seek partnership."

"Others would warn you that we make treacherous partners."

"The same could be said of us. Would you at least hear our proposal?"

"Your craft is puny. We could destroy you easily."

"This is true. And unlike our last encounter, this time we come unarmed. We do not want to destroy another of your ships or another world."

There was a long pause. "How do you propose to make landfall?"

"We need a flat strip of land." We knew how to describe it in common galactic units. "A vehicular road, beach, or desert flat might be available."

"We will contact you on your next orbit." A little over an hour later we received a detailed description of how to get to what turned out to be the roof of a seriously large building. We had to make a couple of folds and fall a bit to get in the right position and then M brought us down, gliding down through the increasingly close-up and detailed images they sent us.

Everyone who greeted us was armed, and there were a lot of them. The raiders weren't quite feline; they were furry and their ancestors obviously carnivorous hunters, but they didn't quite resemble anything familiar. They reminded me more of lemurs than anything else on earth. They all pointed their weapons at us as one of them stepped to the forefront and said, "You say you bring gifts."

Episode 13

The raiders' fur was decorated in a dazzling mix of colors and patterns, and it took a moment for me to realize these were artificial, not natural. The raiders were bipedal, with hands much like our own but oddly cloven feet which were thickly shielded from the ground by some kind of horn or nail shield, and they wore their Mark of the Curators across what a human would call his chest. The colorful patterns carefully avoided the Mark. It was not clear how their weapons worked; they appeared heavy and had roughly the shape of a long gun, but whatever they were it was clear from the way they handled the devices that they could make something bad happen if pointed at you.

I gestured toward the Boxcar and said, "This is our first gift. We give you this starship. It is an example of our craft for you to either use or take apart and inspect as you desire. We place no constraints on this gift."

"Not that you could."

"Of course."

"What do you want in return?"

"We would like to make a proposal to your leaders. This is just the beginning of what we hope might be a long term partnership."

They took us to a place that looked a lot like a hotel, except for the really secure doors and lack of windows. And we were there for awhile. They gave us water and eventually food which was obviously nanite duplication of template stuff we had left behind on the Boxcar, and otherwise we had no communication of any kind with anybody. M worried about that, but I told her they were probably picking the Boxcar apart before deciding whether we were worth an interview. Finally we were summoned.

There were about thirty raiders physically in the room but the real leaders appeared by video. "Your perverse modesty habits give us worry that you might be hiding weapons," the leading physically present raider said with a shrug.

"And we have also been told that you have no Mark of the Curators," one of the leaders said from a large projection screen. "We find this highly unbelievable."

I started to unbutton my shirt but M slapped my hands away. "No J, I got this," she said, and she disrobed, casually tossing her clothes to the corners of the room as if she didn't care if she ever retrieved them. "It's appropriate," she said as she cast off her shirt. "After all I was also naked when I destroyed their ship."

I sucked in my breath, but the aliens didn't react.

"We are more relaxed in our perverse modesty habit when we sleep," she continued. Pants to the other side of the room.

"Our ship *screee* caught you sleeping?"

"Yes. It was an excellently planned attack," she said as she flung her panties away.

"How did you ever prevail?"

"I had programmed my ship to monitor for unexpected fold activity. It woke me up when yours entered the system."

"Your ship can monitor for fold activity without active human operators?"

"Our ships can *fold* without human operators. But in this case all it had to do was get me and J awake and to it before your guys bombed our tent." She let this sink in—as with the Vikings, victory is victory but killing your enemy as they sleep is not exactly glorious. M, now naked, held her hands up and slowly spun around so they could see her from every angle.

"Extraordinary," several voices said from the projectors. And then one: "But you are marked. If not the Curators, how did that happen?"

M displayed her tattoos. "As with everything else, the Curators were useless to us so we have to mark ourselves. We do it by injecting ink into the skin. It's painful but that's part of the meaning. This one is the first combat group I flew with. This one celebrates becoming a test pilot, flying things which might not work as we expect so we can fix them if they don't kill us first. And this one is my first combat kill. It's been awhile since we had a hot war on Earth so that's your ship."

I was not sure this provocation was a good idea, but M is a warrior and her instincts proved true. "It is good that our warriors are remembered," one of the video leaders said.

"So let us hear from your companion, warrior," one of the others said.

M motioned for me to stand back again. "I am a warrior, but J is a diplomat. I trained to kill. He trained to heal, and found himself mixed up in this galactic business. Please don't think of him as a weak person because he hasn't killed a fold ship. In the important ways, the ways that matter most to both of our species, he is stronger than me." And then she waved me on.

"We give you the ship Boxcar which we used to establish our own first beachhead on an undeveloped world. Inside it you will find all the tools and technical manuals necessary to disassemble and maintain it, and samples of the fluids necessary to service and fuel it; your nanites should be able to duplicate you an adequate supply of them. You are welcome to use the ship as it is as we did or pick it apart for its technology. We will answer any technical questions you have for us. Our intention is to keep no secrets of our technology from you."

"The reason we make this offer is that we want you to understand how difficult it would be for you to switch from your established nanite technology to our methods. Our engines and our tiny fold drives are built on generations of work by hundreds of thousands of people, building tools that were used to build tools that were needed to build more tools. Unlike yourselves, we had no nanites so there were many intermediate products we needed which justified this technology as we built it up. There are vast complexes staffed by thousands of humans dedicated to making various small parts of the Boxcar. We think you would find it hard to justify duplicating all that work just to make small fold ships. We could be wrong, in which case we will give you all the help we can. But even with an all out effort by your entire species it would be decades before you are able to make these things without our help."

"But we did not come here to discourage you. We came to offer you the same ability that we have, to independently create colonies for your people on the undeveloped Curated worlds

THE CURATORS

of the galaxy, which greatly outnumber those that have developed. Since your fold ships are too large to land, you need to keep them in orbit if you're not doing a quick raid, and your bottleneck is that you need ground infrastructure to generate power for ground to orbit shuttles. That infrastructure, like the fold ships, is too large to transport to the surface of another world. So you can get there but getting back is not practical."

I reached into my pocket and pulled out a small projector. "If I may," I said. The physically present raiders stiffened but they didn't interfere. I turned it on and projected a picture onto the wall behind me. There were murmurs. I knew this basic Earth consumer tech was far smaller than anything they could make.

"Your power generation technique is clean and elegant, using the fold drive to recycle falling objects past magnetic coils. But it's not very energy dense, so you need a lot of towers. Nanites make such construction practical, but not fast, and the nanites themselves need power to do the construction. These are portable power generating devices that work on a different principle. This station is based on two structures we call shipping containers. They are designed to be transported, and can be parachuted to the surface of a world from a fold ship. They work by using your microfold communication technology to tap energy from the interior of a star, using it to boil water to drive a turbine-driven generator. You are watching a team of six humans assemble these two units into a station that will generate enough power to return a shuttle to orbit in a few days. It will take them four days to get everything hooked up and working."

I let this settle in.

"Unlike the fold drive, this is a technology that is within your immediate reach with nanite tech and tools and parts easily built with nanite tech. We have generations of experience with these steam generators which we will share with you. And while we used the same microfold sunlight power to destroy your ship, this was our first application for the solar microfold. It was the power generator that gave us the idea for the sunlight cannon."

"So you will be giving us your superweapon too," one of the leaders said from a monitor.

"You don't even need us for that. The only secret of the sunlight cannon is that it is possible to make them at all. Making boilers and generators can be a bit tricky though, and we can steer you past a lot of mistakes we made learning those crafts."

From another monitor, "This is an extraordinary offer which seems much more likely to be some kind of trick than to be genuine."

"These are extraordinary times. We reason that if you are busy expanding your culture to new worlds, you will have no need to make war with us on the other side of the galaxy, or even your old neighbors. We have this experience with members of our own species who sometimes became raiders. Buying them off did not work, but accepting them as neighbors and working together with them in partnership did. Within a few generations nobody remembered that our ancestors had once been bitter enemies."

"You have the ship. We make this further offer: We will give you the location of Earth. We have brought the segments of a docking ring which will make it possible for our shuttle to dock with you; mount it to one of your fold ships and send it to Earth. All we ask is that you make stable orbit. We will provide shuttle service for any personnel you wish to send, and we will show them anything they want to see—our production facilities, our transportation infrastructure, our power plants, even our weapons. And we will give them the power generation technology, which was a bit too big to fit in the Boxcar."

I offered the projector to one of the physically present raiders who seemed to be in charge, and they escorted us back to our room. M did not bother to retrieve her clothing, but it was delivered to us in a leather bag a couple of hours later.

We were locked in our suite and had no communications with the outside world, but they treated us decently. After two days a screen lit up and one of the raider leaders addressed us. "We have decided to accept your offer to visit Earth. The fold ship *scree* has just departed with your docking ring in place."

"We were kind of hoping to go with it," I said.

"You should hope this goes well," the raider said. "Whether you ever see your world again depends on the reception we receive from your people."

"Well that's not ominous at all," I said as the screen went dark.

"And not exactly unexpected, either. Vikings, remember?" M said. "Just be glad we're not in chains in a dungeon. Yet."

Episode 14

We were in our comfortable but isolated prison apartment for three more days before there was a knock on the door. They had never knocked before, and we didn't know how to offer entry, but a screen lit up and told us to just say "Open" in English. M said "Open" and a single apparently unarmed raider bowed before crossing the threshold.

"Your colors look familiar," I said. "Weren't you on one of the screens during our presentation?"

"I was indeed, human J. I am *scree* the Praetor of Resources. From our communications we believe your version of me leads what is called your Department of the Interior."

"I thought you were afraid we might have bombs in our clothes," M said.

"Indeed we did. But our welcome at your world has surpassed our every expectation. Your people have extended an unimaginable generosity considering how our species met. And your constructions are said to be awe inspiring. We were very foolish to risk making you enemies. And so the two of you now have the same freedom of our world, and I am tasked to be your guide. Anything you wish to see you may see, anywhere you wish to go you may go, anything you wish to ask will be answered if I can access the answer."

"We don't even know where to begin," I said.

"Truthfully, we know you closely explored the young world Seville, and our technology like most of that in the galaxy is almost exactly the same as theirs. We just use it a bit differently."

"Tactics," M said.

"Quite so, human M. I have also been asked to mention that we know that you are the individual who single-handedly defeated our fold ship in battle. This act commands our deepest respect." She looked at me. "And human J, we are told you are the individual who prevailed on your society to extend the generous offer of your help to colonize undeveloped worlds. We are afraid that this is a debt we may never adequately repay."

"Never attacking us again would be quite adequate repayment," I said.

"My advisors say your facial grimace indicates amusement. It is an amusing observation. But we are as fiercely loyal as we are belligerent, and we will not consider mere peace adequate compensation for what you are offering. We attacked you and then we treated you rudely when you came to us in peace. We seek to rectify that."

"Do you have any natural wonders you are proud of?" M asked. "We have seen much on the planets we have explored, but on Earth we find that things like mountains and waterfalls and volcanoes and glaciers inspire us. As with the technology these might be things found on many worlds, but your examples would be *yours* and worthy of visiting."

So raider N bowed, and we did a little pocket tour of raider world natural wonders. Toward the end of the first day I realized I had been hearing *scree* periodically when she referred to her own world. "Yes, we are told you are also known for naming worlds in your language," she said. "Would you care to name ours?"

"I've actually been thinking about it," I said. "I choose to call your world Kattegat."

"Is there any significance?"

"A thousand years ago there were humans who lived much as your people do, except without space travel it was other humans they raided from the sea. They are considered among the fiercest warriors our kind ever produced. Kattegat was the home village of one of their most successful leaders."

N bowed again. "A name we accept with honor, then," she said. "How did your ancestors deal with the raiders of Kattegat?"

"They were called Vikings. Our world was very fractured—still is actually—and different people reacted to them differently. The most successful offered them land to settle and the hospitality of neighbors. Within a few generations nobody remembered that their ancestors had once been bitter enemies."

"It is not just your constructions that are awe-inspiring," N said. "It is said that in our deep past we turned against ourselves as you describe, but with our Curation we turned our aggression outward toward other races on other worlds. But your memory of that era is relatively fresh, and you have applied that same lesson to interstellar relations. We may have much to learn from you."

We were in something like an airport, and another raider approached us. His gait was halting and his fur was spotty, and I realized he must have been very old. "I need to introduce you to this fellow," N said. "He is one of our most renowned artists."

"If I may," the stranger said. "Would you extend some part of your bare skin you don't mind if it might be stained for a few *scree*?"

M and I looked at one another and she said, "Renowned artist, eh?" and stuck out her forearm. He applied a few dots of color to her skin. I followed suit.

"I need to make sure there is no irritation, and that the removal process works as intended," he said before retreating.

"What was that about?" M asked when he was gone.

"It could be a very big deal if it is workable," was all N said.

A couple of hours later after we visited an active volcano and returned, the same individual returned and swabbed our skin with what smelled for all the world like rubbing alcohol, and the dots of color came off. He seemed very satisfied. "I will see you again soon," he said.

"I did ask what that was about, didn't I?" M said.

"He's an artist. He now knows he might have a canvas."

The next day N properly introduced us to the colorist. "You have probably noticed we wear colored patterns in our fur. We would feel odd—perhaps as you do without clothes—without these patterns. They honor our ancestors and our own accomplishments and proclaim our identity. Our colors give us courage in battle. O is our most senior and accomplished colorist. For years our top leaders would only accept color from him. *Scree* ago he retired, and hasn't given color for many years. But he asked us for an audience with you."

The old raider bowed and said, "I humbly request the honor of giving you color," he said. "It would mean a great deal to my people, particularly those who lost family on the fold ship *scree*. Color honors the dead and celebrates victory. Color cements truce. We know your ways are very different but for our own people, accepting color would be a great step toward unity between our species."

"So this is what the color daubs were about?"

"Yes, I would not offer this if I thought it would harm you, or considering your ways if I wasn't sure I could remove the color after an appropriate period of time."

"What would you consider an appropriate period of time?"

"A day would be sufficient," O said. "If you are willing more would honor us."

"Well I'm in," M said without hesitation. "What about you, J"

"I'm a bit reluctant to..."

"If I might offer a suggestion, it might be useful for one of you to continue to exhibit your modesty habit," N said. "All of our people will be watching this, and most of them don't know about that."

I glanced back at M and wondered if she realized she wasn't just offering to be naked, she was offering to be naked on planetwide an possibly galactic TV. But I just said "Could you just color the parts of my body I normally expose, like my face and hands?"

"I can work with that," O said.

Later I said to M, "You do realize that if they broadcast this globally the chances of it eventually reaching Earth are something like one hundred percent."

She shrugged. "Sure, but I think one of us has to do it, and have you noticed that all the aliens we have met so far have rigid or bony penises? If you go naked I think you'll end up spending the whole show explaining how your dick works. And face it, when *that* got back to Earth it would be a bit more humiliating than me becoming a pinup model."

Two days later we were standing just offstage as we listened to a Kattegat media personality introduce us. It was weirdly familiar, but also oddly nostalgic because the large cameras and manual controls for everything gave the studio an Earth-1970's feel. We were given to understand that nearly everyone on the planet was watching, and there was a live audience of several hundred individuals. M and I both wore mikes and earphones for the translators, which were powered by their vast and deeply buried supercomputer complexes, and M was naked to display the colors O had given her.

"Our visitors from Earth," we heard in our earpieces, and at this cue we walked onstage and bowed toward the host and then toward his audience both in-house and global.

Episode 15

As we walked onstage a thunderous roar filled the studio. The audience were stomping the floor with their naturally hard soled feet, and the floor was wood so it made quite a racket. In fact, I realized that the entire building seemed to be made of wood, as were many of the other Kattegatian structures we had seen on our tour. Being used to our extensive use of wood on Earth I had failed to notice how sharply this contrasted with both Seville and Pompeii, where almost everything was made of nanite matrices.

"We have a very unusual show today," the host said with a flourish that could have been taken directly from Earth late night TV. "Our guests tonight are aliens who crossed the entire galaxy to find us, despite having never ventured more than a few hundred light-years from their home world before. Our guests have only had the fold drive for a few years, and space travel of any kind for only a few generations. Almost within living memory they did not have electric power or powered transport, yet today they cross the galaxy in craft they build themselves."

There was polite stomping.

"There are a couple of other things you need to know about our guests, who call themselves humans and their world Earth.

THE CURATORS 93

As you can see from the female who graciously offered to wear and display colors for us, they have no Mark of the Curators. Although the Earth itself was apparently Curated, being typical of a world shaped to host life, the ancestors of humans themselves haven't been Curated for some time. They have achieved all of their accomplishments without any of the usual help—no gifts of fire or agriculture or writing or steam power or electric theory, and no nanites. They had to build it all themselves."

This elicited a different reaction from the audience, a collective gasp of surprise.

"I know what you're thinking. Nobody has ever heard of an uncurated species with language or civilization much less space travel before. Well, we have now. Our first encounter with humans was with these two individuals, our present day guests. This was their fold ship." On the monitors we saw the broadcast image change to a picture of the Grasshopper in space. The fold ship we destroyed must have gotten it to them in the last moments before its destruction.

Another audience gasp. "Kattegatians, this is the human fold ship Small Hopping Insect."

This time the audience reaction was different still. It was bewilderment.

"Human J, you named this craft didn't you? Would you care to tell us the significance?"

"Certainly. Thank you for your welcome, by the way. Grasshopper is capable of taking off from the surface of a world, flying high enough on its air breathing engines to fold safely away, and dropping into the atmosphere and landing with its air-breathing engines on another world. It doesn't need surface infrastructure to do any of this."

At this the audience started stomping. This was something anyone in the galaxy would recognize as extraordinary.

"There's *much* more," the host said. "Being raiders, when we learned the humans were building craft like this, we wanted one for ourselves for obvious reasons. And what do we do when we want something on Kattegat?"

The audience enthusiastically shouted in unison, and the translator dryly said: "We raid."

"And that is precisely what we did. And you might wonder, since we crossed the galaxy to steal their technology, why M and J are sitting here in a broadcast studio instead of in a cell being interrogated as alien prisoners."

The audience murmured in confusion.

"The Small Hopping Insect wasn't just equipped with a fold drive. It was *armed*. While they were sleeping it autonomously woke them up and warned them that we were coming so they could escape our surprise attack, and when we gave chase... well, Human M, this was your triumph, was it not? Why don't you tell us what happened next?"

M, who was naked in a building full of aliens, told them, "I fired on them with the sunlight cannon and fatally damaged their ship. As they fell toward the ground, since they did not have orbital velocity, my fold drive alerted me to anomalous fold activity and I folded us out just in time to watch them fold the entire planet into its host star."

The audience gasped, and there were some growls of anger.

"I'm sorry about the loss of your ship and your people," M continued. "But I think your own people would say that if

THE CURATORS

someone comes after you, you will do whatever you have to to escape and hit back."

The host made a gesture toward the audience, and they began stomping in rhythmic unison. "Humans, this is how we express respect toward those who have earned it." The stomping turned more chaotic, like the applause we had heard earlier.

"And there is *even more* to this extraordinary story. The humans took the trouble to find us, but when our guests came they did not bring their superweapon. This is what happened."

On the monitors they played the tape of our initial encounter after landing, when I told them the fold ship Boxcar was a gift and that we wished to be allies. This left the audience staring in dumbfounded silence.

"Would you care to explain why any species, much less two individuals such as yourselves, responds to an attempt to raid and kill you with such generosity?"

"I reasoned that if you wanted our technology so badly you must have some good reason. There is no shortage of resources in the galaxy, but we knew from our short association with a couple of other Curated races that there is a shortage of ways to reach those resources on worlds that aren't already developed. We came to offer you such a method so you wouldn't feel the need to try taking ours again. We knew it would be very hard for you to duplicate our industries so we came up with something easier for you to use with your existing nanite tech."

"And so they did! As we broadcast our fold ship *scree* is in stable orbit around the Earth and humans have been providing transport for our research teams for several days now. They have generously offered us everything we need to colonize undeveloped worlds on our own, without their future assistance, and to bring resources home in whatever quantity we desire."

There was stomping applause but I think still a bit of puzzlement in the audience. "Our away teams have sent us some holiday snaps," the host said, and I wondered what human had taught the translator that phrase. "Take a look."

The first picture was of the Manhattan skyline. "This is just one human city," the host said. "Some of those buildings are over eighty levels tall. The tallest that can safely be built with nanites are about twenty levels, and those sacrifice a lot of floor area to structural support. There are hundreds of cities that look like this on Earth."

There was stomping. "These skyscrapers are built on skeletons of pure metal." Switch to picture of a foundry pouring liquid steel. "Humans melt and brute-shape metal on a scale that we can barely imagine. You might wonder where the power to do this comes from." Switch to picture of the Hoover Dam. "Some of it comes from works like this, which exploit water pressure from hydrological runoff." Picture of conventional power plant. "Most comes from these, which use fire to boil water to turn electrical generators." Picture of solar cell field. "But while that technology built their society it has created problems, and now much of their power comes from resources like these, directly turning sunlight into electricity..." Picture of a windmill farm. "...or wind. These wind turbines are miracles in their own right, almost as tall as the sky buildings and they would be impossible to build with nanites."

The audience was completely silent.

"None of this explains their aircraft or tiny fold drives though. This is the other end of human technological prowess."

Picture of the Boeing assembly plant with a couple of Dreamliners in the foreground. "This place makes aircraft, which use fire to propel themselves through the atmosphere like enormous birds. So far every human starship has been a converted aircraft." Picture of another large industrial building. "This place makes electronic circuit wafers." Picture of the inside, with clean room protocols being observed. "All dust has to be removed from the air, and the precision employed is unimaginable. Thousands of these facilities produce billions of products per day. We may lament our scarcity of resources, but nobody in the galaxy has ever seen industrial works like those of Earth."

The audience began rhythmically stomping, the sign of respect. "After the intermission, we will get more personal with these beings who crossed the galaxy to show generosity after we tried to kill them."

"I didn't think you had a capitalist system," I told the host when we were off-air. "What is the purpose of the break?"

"We will show what I believe your people call public service advisories. It gives the away audience a chance to attend to personal business, and us a chance to make small corrections." While we were off-air the colorist O was escorted onstage and seated next to us.

"I hope your colors are wearing well," he said to M.

"Just fine," she said.

We couldn't read the countdown but the translator alerted us that it was nearing zero. "Welcome back," the host said. "We are now joined by one of our most renowned artists, the fur colorist O. Welcome back, sir."

"It's been awhile," O said.

"It's been *scree* since you retired from offering color. I don't guess I have to ask why you came back?"

"It has been many generations since a colorist has had the opportunity to color an opponent who defeated us in battle. Human M has offered me a great privilege which I humbly hope I have fulfilled."

"Since you colored her whole body I suppose you can verify she has no Mark of the Curators?"

"That is true. And in private, her companion allowed me to examine him too. We all know the Curators embed their mark deeply and it is hard to completely obscure. We also have confirmation from the genetic scans they allowed at our request. It has been millions of *scree* since the Curators touched the humans' ancestors."

"If I may take an aside, this privacy thing is interesting. Human J, you wear garments to obscure your body. Care to explain that to us?"

"Our modesty habit goes back to our earliest history. On earth we actually have laws requiring the use of clothes to obscure parts of our bodies from public view."

"Whatever for?"

"Well, clothing turns out to be useful; like your fur colors it can display status or personal style, and it can also protect against the environment. Because we wear clothing we can comfortably live in some of the most hostile environments on Earth. And even in mild climates, our ancestors apparently found constant exposure to sexual temptation distracting."

"But surely that would only be a factor when you are in season? We have a rich genre of anecdotes about what a mistake it is to trust ourselves to do anything important when we are in season."

M and I looked at one another and couldn't help laughing. "How often are you folks in season?"

"About one month per year. Fortunately we learned to stagger our seasons long ago using hormones so we aren't all crazy and unreliable at the same time."

M and I looked at one another and broke out in giggles. "Your expressions indicate mirth," the host said. "What's so funny?"

"Humans are always in season," M said.

Eyes went wide with astonishment throughout the studio. "You mean that right now, the two of you, you could theoretically..."

"There's nothing theoretical about it."

"But surely you aren't fertile all the time."

"No, naturally females like myself are fertile a few days per month. But males are always fertile and we are all always ready to mate even when the female isn't fertile. Our biologists believe evolution selected this for social reasons, but it became a problem when we invented cities. Most of our closest animal relatives are more like yourselves."

"This is amazing. I wasn't given this in prep. You built the most ambitious tech in the galaxy in just a couple of generations despite being constantly distracted by sexual feelings?"

"Well, now you know why we normally wear clothes," I said. Some of the audience actually stomped at that.

"But you have agreed to be naked for us," the host said to M. "We do understand this is rather unusual for humans."

"Well, it was necessary to give O a proper canvas. And honestly, I would feel a lot less safe doing this on Earth. Here I understand nobody is sexually distracted by my body."

"Not exactly nobody," I said with a small snicker.

"I plan to mate with you anyway," she said matter-of-factly. "I don't need everyone in broadcast range getting the same idea."

"Wow," the host said. "Well, colorist O, can you top that by explaining your designs?"

"I doubt it," O said with a rumble we had been coached to understand was their form of laughter. "I colored M's entire body, of course, and J allowed me his head and hands according to his race's more typical modesty habit. I started them both off the same, with the burst of light on the upper right of the face, titanium white to illustrate the ray of their Sunlight Cannon." O motioned for M to stand up. "Across the front of her body we have M's training. She is quite an heroic figure, having risked her life to test machinery that might not work. Human technology is so new that fatal failures happen with some frequency. And on her back, the Sunlight Cannon hits our fold ship *scree*. In its death throes it transitions to her thighs, where I placed the streak of the Small Hopping Insect's last-moment escape and the bright-rimmed blackness of destruction as the world beneath them was folded into its star."

There was generous stomping.

"For J, having only his face and hands to work with, I also started with the Sunlight Cannon on his face. But in his case his hands are green with life, representing the extraordinary human forgiveness and generosity and the new potential for our own species which our alliance may portend. As an artist I find it very beautiful that both of these outcomes emerge from the same violent origin."

"Thank you, O," the host said. "For our last segment I have a connection to our Praetor of Resources N, who has been escorting our human guests for the last few days. Praetor N are you with us?"

"So I am," a voice replied. The broadcast screens showed a still picture of N and a transcription in alien type, and M and I got voice translations in English in our earphones, as we were used to by now.

"Praetor, what is your impression of the humans?"

"Well I have only dealt directly with your guests, but I am also in touch with our away team at Earth and can say they have seen much more than you have been able to show your audience. We are learning to melt metals, to make pressure vessels and precision bearings and a few other things we need to make small portable power stations. They have even offered to trade with us for these finished goods until we have our own manufacturing up to speed. So we anticipate that we will begin exploration not to raid but to colonize new worlds within a month or two."

At this the studio erupted in stomping which the host allowed to go on for some time. The host and O even joined in the stomping. M and I bowed repeatedly, which we had been coached was the polite response to such praise.

Finally the host gestured for quiet. "M and J, what are your own personal plans for the future?"

"We had been hoping to go home with your fold ship," M said. "But your security people had different ideas."

Praetor N was still on the line. "We did not know what our reception would be like at Earth," he said. "If we had known we would have sent you along. But if you do want to get home soon, may I offer a proposal? Some of us would like to try out your gift to us, the fold ship Square Shipping Conveyance. Would you be willing to take some of us home with you and show us how to fly it?"

I deferred to M, and she bowed and said "We would be honored."

Episode 16

For a moment I thought I would be making some pancakes with M after we returned to our quarters, but it turned out there was a raider waiting for us there.

"I apologize for the intrusion," she said with a small bow.

"That's okay, we just didn't realize you would be here."

"That's because your hosts don't know. I know my colleague told you we walk among all of our children. Even among the miscreants such as these—and, some would say, yourselves."

"You're a Curator? Aren't the raiders listening in on us?"

"Oh, of course they are, but it's trivial for us to defeat such measures. They think you are quietly watching a recording of your own show."

"To what do we owe the honor, then?" M asked.

"There are those among us who think we should have revealed ourselves to our children aeons ago. The argument against this was that it would break the stability of our galactic garden. But now that the stability of our garden is in jeopardy anyway, those voices are more active and one result is that we are making these contacts with you humans. I believe my colleague imparted to J what a departure this is in all of our long history."

"So he did," I said. "Of course there is a way for you to protect the stability of your garden. I believe he said you resorted to it in the distant past."

"If you refer to folding your world into your star, that is the *last* thing we would contemplate. Even the raiders do not disappoint us. The fact that they have managed to make so much trouble for the last seven hundred thousand of your years makes them one of our more interesting families, and it's why we are inclined to forgive them this once for destroying our handiwork."

"Why do the raiders make so much trouble? Why do they raid?"

"We developed their world because this star has what your people call sufficient metallicity to support complex life, but it and its system are deficient in heavier elements such as iron and nickel which are necessary to make nanites. They had enough resources to build a civilization and get into space, but not to build an entire world civilization according to normal standards. You have probably noticed their extensive use of native materials for architecture. When they saw the works of our other children they became envious and decided that taking was an appropriate way to augment what we had denied them."

"And we are giving them a great power."

"And we find it a very interesting development. You humans developed because we denied you gifts. The raiders developed because we denied them resources. You now offer them ready access to the resources they have lusted after for longer than your kind have existed. And you will find that they will probably repay you by forwarding a gift or two of ours in your direction. One reason for this visit is to assure you that this does not bother us. In fact, we are watching your relationship develop with fascination. It is so rare for us to observe a new thing in our garden."

"Well it worked out pretty well considering the whole gunpoint and hostage way it started out," M said.

"I suppose it doesn't matter now to let you know that while we wanted to see how you would handle it without knowing, we were closely monitoring you all the way. We really were unsure how they would react to you, and from the moment of your arrival we had you in focus to fold you out of any situation that turned dangerous. You didn't need our assistance though and handled your introduction brilliantly. That broadcast was genius, and you wear raider colors well, human M."

"I had the best artist," she said.

"Indeed. I think I have made all the points I needed to and you have a flight to prepare for. I know you are the junior species but you have learned much more than most of our other children. Teach them with wisdom." And with that, the Curator bowed and vanished.

"I don't think I am ever going to get used to them doing that," M said. Then she put on her flight jumpsuit.

The Boxcar was not the same as it was when we left it. The raiders had installed twelve seats in the cargo space. The seats were made of nanite matrix and loosely based on the pilot and copilot seats, with safety belts even, but the makers had obviously realized their material was not as strong as pure aluminum and had thickened most of the struts. They had also plated much of the floor, even through the cockpit, which seemed strangely unnecessary.

Raider P showed us the changes; it seems she was an experienced foldship pilot who was supposed to learn to fly the Boxcar. M indicated that she would then be taking the copilot's seat. They looked back at me, and I claimed what would have been new raider seat 1A on a domestic airliner for myself.

For the flight we were joined by several raider big cheeses including Praetor of Resources N. It turned out the surface we had landed on was actually the roof of a fold power station, composed of thousands of internal columns where magnetic weights were continually dropped past coils and folded back to the top to generate electricity. The top was completely flat and smooth and several kilometers on edge.

Praetor N was seated next to me as M taxied off. "I have been given to understand that your world is poor in nanite resources," I said. "This facility must have been a challenge to build."

N appeared surprised for a moment, then just nodded. "We had to be very creative mixing native resources in with the nanite structure and functionality in order to make it possible," he said. "Most races just sit the bucket out in a field and tell it to start building. It was much more difficult for us."

M was pointing out instruments to P, and then she throttled forward and we were all pressed back into our seats. Then Boxcar lifted off, and M punched us upward.

"That was dramatic," someone behind me said.

"You have done this before?" Praetor N asked me.

"Oh, many times. We're used to it."

"It seems rather erratic."

"Well, we're being supported by the atmosphere, and the atmosphere is erratic." We circled and rose as M showed more of the controls to P, and finally had P engage some controls on the new fold interface and punch the execute button. Through the windows we could see that we jumped upward about a kilometer.

M hit the intercom. "We are now going to do a series of short fold maneuvers designed to limit the amount of your atmosphere we lose irretrievably to outer space in the course of leaving. We will fold, glide for a bit as the bubble of dense air dissipates, then fold upward again until the atmosphere is too thin to be worth bothering with. Strap in, as we will soon be weightless."

I made a point of checking my seatbelt but saw that Praetor N was just flashing what for a raider would be considered a wicked grin.

The Boxcar jumped and jumped again, ten times, and finally M hit the intercom and said "Well folks we're in space now and we still have interior gravity. I suppose somebody did a few tweaks on our ship."

"Just a little gravity plating," a voice behind me said. "Your specifications said its deadweight would be within the ship's limits."

"And so it is," M said. "This will pleasantly improve our experience as we fall toward Neptune to adjust our velocity." Our outward trip had allowed M to calibrate the drive so it only took us two more jumps to cross the galaxy and start that process. As she was showing this to student pilot P, P said something very loud in the growling raider language which the translator reported as "You have got to be introducing me to a coitally novel experience."

"How so?" M asked.

"For us to cross the galaxy requires at least twenty folds, each followed by a careful orientation to keep us synchronized with the map. Since the Curator map only shows developed worlds we have to use them as way points. If we tried to do this all in one step we'd end up hopelessly lost at the far end with no way to figure out which nearby star is yours. We might be off by dozens or even hundreds of light-years."

"Well our instruments are precise enough to put us within a light-year or two if we're well oriented. They weren't calibrated well enough to do that on our trip out, but they are now. And if we're too far out for Sol to be the brightest star in the sky, spectra are pretty definite and we know our own home."

"You have the equipment to identify spectra on this tiny ship?"

"It's even all automated. You just punch the destination coordinates in through that panel." M showed P how to do it. "And press ENTER."

P pressed ENTER and we folded. The ship did an automatic destination scan and after about fifteen seconds it beeped. "About a light-year off," M said. "See, there's Sol." There was excited muttering among the passengers.

"Since it knows Sol's luminosity it has now positively located and oriented us, just press ENTER again to proceed to the intended coordinates," M said.

"This thing doesn't even need a pilot," she responded.

"Well, for folding it really doesn't. Our first fold experiment was a remote robot to remove the chance of accidentally folding Earth into Sol, and computers are better at this stuff than we are anyway."

"*Your* computers might be," P said. Soon we were falling toward Neptune to match our velocity to that of the Earth.

Then it developed that having anticipated a much longer trip, the raiders had brought snacks. I was still a bit dubious about their food, although they said their genetic scan positively showed what was safe for humans to eat. But they also brought alcohol. The fermented beverage had a strange but not unpleasant taste and I thought there would probably be quite a market for it on Earth. And with the gravity plating in place we drank out of ordinary cups instead of squeeze bulbs.

Once we weren't going stupidly fast M showed P how to fold us over to Earth and make the fine adjustments so we could drop into the atmosphere. M herself landed us, showing P each maneuver necessary to do it safely.

Once the craft was at rest P said "You have got to be drop-out-of-the-sky-and-bomb-it kidding me. There is no way I will ever be able to do that without wrecking the craft."

"I wasn't born knowing how to land an airplane," M said. "We have classes. In fact we have specific classes for this donor aircraft, the C130. Get some pilots together and we'll train you as a group."

The Director was waiting for us as we exited the aircraft. The raiders went off to meet the others who had come before them on the fold ship. "We didn't expect you to bring it back," he said.

"Well, I think the idea is to get them in shape to fly it back themselves. They're going to need some aircraft flying lessons."

"I'll arrange it. By the way, those are nice tats guys. I hope they come off."

"Isopropyl alcohol," M said.

"Over how much of your body?"

"One hundred percent."

He looked at me. "Just my face and hands. But M looked really good on planetary TV," I said.

"I know I'm going to find out but I don't think I want to know."

"Hey, it was fun. They don't see us as sex objects. I was just a warrior being honored the way they do it. For real."

"Okay, that must have been refreshing."

"Very," M said.

Unlike the Sevillians the raiders emptied their fold ship of all but a skeleton crew and so they were all over the Earth, auditing college courses and touring industrial facilities and taking samples and raw materials back to their ship via our shuttle. A lot of humans took an interest in their rich lore of battle stories and some of them became media stars. In turn a few of the raiders took a deep interest in our history instead of our technology. And true to the promise we had made, we hid nothing from them.

At one meet and greet one of the raider visitors introduced himself to me and asked, "I have been intensely curious to ask why you named our homeworld after a body of water."

"I named it after the home village of that Ragnar Viking guy," I said.

At this he dissolved into the apparent coughing fit I'd learned to recognize as raucous raider laughter. "Ragnar Lothbrok almost certainly existed in real life," he informed me, "But no town of Kattegat ever did. Kattegat is the ocean strait that separates Sweden and Denmark. Apparently the people who made that entertainment show just liked the name, but it actually means, 'small domestic animal neck' and refers to the difficulty of navigating the sea lane."

"Okay, so how did you find this out from a hundred thousand light years away?"

"Oh, I just got back from Norway. By the way, the Norwegians all think you're an idiot."

At that we laughed and shared a round of drinks. "They gave me a tour," he said after our first toast. "At least you named our home after a very beautiful and strategically important body of water."

I talked with him for several more hours. The raiders were as fascinated with our closeness to our own history as many humans were with their exploits as space Vikings.

M and I wore our colors for a month. After washing them off we went back to what we had been doing before the raiders attacked us, scouting for new colonies and providing support for those already started. Raider pilot P got her pilot's license and became confident enough to pilot the Boxcar back to Kattegat. And soon after the first raider fold ship folded home, a new one appeared.

When the news arrived two months later that the raiders had used the Boxcar to set up their first colony in their part of the galaxy, millions of humans celebrated with them.

Episode 17

Four Years Later

Our human-form Curator became a regular visitor to our house, particularly after M and I got married. He revealed himself to the Director who in turn directed us to be his liaison with our species, and to keep it all very quiet. As far as anyone else knew he was a human engineer who occasionally did contract work for projects at the base.

There were now thousands of raiders permanently living on Earth and hundreds of humans on Kattegat and its new colonies. While M and I weren't the first human couple to exchange vows on another world the raiders did offer us the opportunity to do it further from home than anyone else would for awhile, on their newest and most distant colony. Being undeveloped it offered us a honeymoon of exploring and sleeping beneath the stars not too different from our experience when we first met the raiders on the occasion of their surprise attack. But now the raiders and humans were allies and trading partners and our alliance was considered strong by both sides.

The rest of the galaxy was mostly unthrilled, but there was a sigh of relief on the other side of the galaxy that the raiders didn't seem inclined to do much raiding any more now that they had colonies. A few races had expressed displeasure that they were getting gifts of technology from us humans that nobody else enjoyed, and one race that in particular spun that feeling to white-hot hatred was the Sevillians, who now blamed themselves for discovering us and bringing us into the galactic community at all.

The raiders had partially repaid us for our generosity with samples of gravity plating, but three years of research had made little progress toward understanding how it worked. Unlike the fold drive, which all developed races mostly understood, all the raiders or anyone else really knew about gravity plating it was that certain nanites made it work. So part of our trade was components and raw materials for nanite-based gravity plating. We were still nervous about setting up nanite based manufacturing on Earth, where it might fall into unreliable hands.

Our Curator knocked precisely at eight on Friday as he'd been doing for over two years. It's easy to be punctual when you can instantly transport yourself to any place on Earth, or for that matter on numerous other inhabited worlds orbiting other stars.

"I received a communication today," he said as M set out dinner. "One of our agents on Seville has been observing a construction project they are undertaking in orbit. It is unusually large for something that hasn't been announced to the general population." He used his hand to project an image on the wall of our dining room. It shifted indicating progress over time. "We are fairly sure this first stage is a fold drive," he said. "But look what it is now becoming."

The structure built around the fold drive was barely larger than the fold drive and its power source together. It had no windows or obvious bays. It was a tiny fraction of the size of any alien fold ship we'd ever seen, though still larger than most human fold ships. Yet it was taking on an appearance of completion; it did not seem they were planning to build it any bigger.

"They are making two of these. Sorry about the quality of the images but even with our technology, these are still telescopic images from the ground."

"I wish P were here," M said. "I'd have an interesting question to ask her about nanite based fold drives."

The Curator smiled. "Who do you think makes those drives possible? I can probably answer your question."

"The reason these fold drives can't be remotely controlled is that they have to be carefully calibrated to set the range and aperture, right?"

"Yes, you have automated those functions but none of our other children have ever managed to do that."

"But if you wanted to *deliberately* fold a world into its sun, you just massively detune it, right? You could automate *that*."

"The thought had occurred to us," he said, "but we considered it so monstrous that we..."

M dove for the telephone and hit the top speed-dial setting. "Code ternary burn omaha, get him online *now*," M said. A few moments later: "Director, is the fold span limiter operating?" Pause. "Make sure it is online and stays online. This is the most important thing ever. I'll explain in a bit."

"Surely you don't think they would really..."

"Those aren't ships," M said very definitely. "Those are planet killers."

"If you are right it would be... unfortunate."

THE CURATORS

M poured wine all around. "Sure I hope I'm wrong," M said, "but I don't think I am. Remember I have devoted my life to the arts of war. And J and I have seen what a fold drive can do firsthand. Humans may not have been in space very long but we've been waging war at sea for centuries. And those aren't ships or even submarines. Those are torpedoes."

"Do the Sevillians know we have the fold span limiter?" I asked, genuinely not being in the loop.

"Not by us," M said, and looked at the Curator. "I am pretty sure they don't know," he said. "But I only found out about this business a couple of months ago. Our agent on Seville didn't realize the potential implications until then. This is still a very large project involving transport of a lot of mass to orbit. The nanite fold drive itself is a huge solid mass and its construction is much of the difficulty of building even a normal scale fold ship. To hide something on this scale from the local population is very hard. Our agent would have missed it if we didn't have a superior ability to detect fold activity."

"The question is how close are these things to completion."

We talked some more, and then the Curator sat up very straight. "I have just received a communication from our agent on Seville. The artifacts have disappeared, coincident with the unannounced departure of their fold ship Rate of Change, which was supposedly being refitted."

"That's the submarine," M said as she hit the speed dial again. "Ternary burn omaha, yeah I know, it's me again. Director, they're on their way. Is there any unusual fold activity in the Solar System?" Pause. "Okay, we'll be there as soon as possible."

"What?"

"An alien fold ship just folded into the Oort cloud. Looks like it's positioning to use Uranus for velocity adjustment. We need to get to the base."

"I can help with that," the Curator said. "Hold hands and stand close to me." We did as instructed. "You might want to close your eyes." We did, and when we opened them we were all at the base, in a vacant office near the Director's.

"Do what you have to do," the Curator said. "I'll be learning what I can. I'll be in touch." And he disappeared.

"I thought you were at home," the Director said when we burst into his office.

"We were about a minute ago. Tonight is our meeting with you-know-who, remember?"

"Okay, this better be good."

Fortunately the Curator had flashed his images over to M's phone. There was an incoming phone call. "They're at Uranus. Looks like they are aiming for Low Earth Orbit in about an hour and a half."

"How can you tell it's LEO?" I asked. "Why would they bother matching velocity at all?"

"We can tell the vector they're choosing to fall on pretty accurately. We're not just sensing from Earth. We have fold monitors at all the gas giants."

"And this is a very expensive weapon for them to make," M added. "They won't take a chance on it misfiring during a short flyby if they don't have to."

"They put a lot of work into this thing. We have to make sure that work comes to nothing. We've got an hour and a half to figure out what to do."

"Go blast them," one of the assistants said.

"They almost certainly have the sunlight cannon themselves now," M said. "And their ships are a lot better shielded than ours by their sheer mass."

"Do nothing," I said.

Everyone looked at me.

"We have the span limiter and they don't know we have it. They'll drop their torpedo and run, thinking it will obliterate us a few seconds later. Then we go up and carve the torpedo up at our leisure."

"I think this is the best strategy," the Director said, and M nodded. "It's also likely to confuse the attackers because they won't know why their weapon didn't work."

So an hour and a half later we were all still in place when the Sevillian foldship Rate of Change dropped its payload in a stable polar orbit around Earth and then folded off toward, as far as we could tell, nowhere. Seconds later a klaxon sounded. "Span limiter activity," one of the assistants shouted.

"What happens when the span limiter limits one of these things?" I asked M.

"It depends on the fold geometry of the detuned drive. It could fold itself into the Sun, or the fold could just fail." After a few moments the klaxon blew again. "It's still up there and it's retrying."

"Well we can't just leave the fucking thing up there," the Director said. "Any ideas?"

"It's probably otherwise unmanned and unarmed. I can take Grasshopper and blast it to shreds."

"Those shreds will still be the heaviest things that ever reentered from orbit eventually. They could wipe out a city or start a tsunami."

"Well we have the ability to manually adjust the fold aperture radius now, use Grasshopper to fold the whole damn thing back to the Oort cloud."

"The radius of operation of the span limiter is only about an AU. You fold it too far away from Earth it will fold itself and whatever folded it away into the Sun, along with who knows what else. Plus we can't be sure how its detuned fold attempts would affect a calibrated fold."

"Maybe we're overthinking this a bit," I said. "Don't we still have hydrogen bombs? The thing is less than fifty meters across. We should be able to *vaporize* it."

The Director just looked at a guy in uniform who immediately said "On it."

"Sir, there's another problem," M said. "The Sevillians built two of these damn things."

"And you think you know what they're going to do with the other one?"

"I would bet a huge pile of money it's on its way to Kattegat."

Episode 18

The Grasshopper was deemed an inadequate vehicle for our mission to save Kattegat. Since we were going to war we needed something tough, maneuverable and mechanically simple and with room for a possible payload, so we were assigned the C130 based Mail Service. It had essentially been converted to live up to its name, doing package deliveries to the colonies, but it was armed with the sunlight cannon and its fold drive had been calibrated for long-range service by aligning it with Grasshopper's. Instead of a chemical rocket RCS it sported a new microfold-sunlight reaction system which used water superheated by the same process as the power generators and sunlight cannon to produce significant thrust and impulse. It was a cargo model with a large cargo area and the usual C130 big rear door, and when we got to it we found a uniformed Air Force captain waiting for us by a rather provocative object which was mounted in the cargo hold for transport.

"Is that what it looks like?" M asked incredulously. It was about six feet long and conical, tapering from a base about a half a meter across to a rounded tip.

"Of course. It's your hydrogen bomb. To be precise a W-88 ICBM re-entry vehicle with a yield of about 500 kilotons. We have hot-wired this one for you with a simple timer to bypass the Permissive Action Link, which I have been instructed to show you how to use. Congratulations, you two are now a nuclear power."

"And everyone is cool with this?"

"Doctor J, I believe you suggested this yourself and the President has signed off on it. We are committed to doing everything we can to prevent the destruction of any inhabited world, not just Earth."

As he was showing us how to program the bomb timer our Curator showed up. "I've been told you are cleared for everything," our instructor said without elaboration, and he continued our instruction.

"I don't know what we're supposed to do with it. We have no way to launch it on an intercept course without being detected and evaded and maybe destroyed in the process."

"That much is correct," the Curator said. "We are now certain the Rate of Change is armed with a primitive version of your sunlight cannon, and due to its heavier construction you would not prevail in a sunlight cannon battle. If you get much closer than an astronomical unit to them via your fold drive they will detect your presence and be able to either engage you or flee."

"Then like I said, what are we supposed to do with this?"

"My people may be able to give you some assistance. Take this." He offered us what looked for all the world like a locket. "When you get within a couple of light-years of Kattegat and your relative velocity less than about 50 kilometers per second—your calibrated fold drive should be capable of doing that from Neptune in one fold—open this and press the button. This will alert our agent on Kattegat of your arrival. We are setting up a strategy as you fly."

Ten minutes later we were in the air. Thirty minutes later we were falling toward Neptune, and seven hours later M opened the locket and pressed the button.

Within moments we were joined by a Raider. But when this raider spoke, its translator just put out English without any raider growling to translate. "We have met before," she said. "I am one who walks among our children."

"You were watching over us on our last visit to Kattegat," M said.

"Exactly. This is quite a situation. We would resolve it ourselves, but long ago we gave up the building of ships and so while our command of the fold is very accurate, we have become a bit limited in the ability to fold larger objects and dependent on folding to an inhabitable space. Thank you for bringing one."

"Hey, it's the least we could do," I said. "How are we going to do this?"

"We are tracking the Rate of Change as it approaches. It has to use inhabited worlds as way points and we walk among our children with our fold detectors on all of those worlds. We anticipate it to arrive here in about another eight hours. They aren't stopping to lick the *scree*. It should appear within ten to fifteen light-years of us, and they will have to do another reckoning before folding over to one of the Kattegat system's gas giants to correct velocity. We should have about twenty minutes to act."

The raider described the plan to us, and M said it was a thing of martial beauty. "Even with our superior technology we are out-armored, outgunned, and cannot fold very close without blowing our cover," she said. "If they don't destroy us they simply fold away before we can do anything. But *this* is a plan."

Later, the raider simply said, "They are here. Range point seven light years." Our fold drive control console lit up and coordinates entered themselves.

"How did you do that..." M said.

"Just execute the fold. I could do it myself but you are the captain of this vessel. It will put us about one point five AU from the Rate of Change, outside of their detection radius for your fold drive."

M executed the fold. At this range the alien ship still wasn't even visible, but the raider knew exactly where it was. "Our time is short," she said. "And I need a bit of it," she said closing her eyes.

"What are you doing?"

"Feeling the interior layout of the Sevillian ship."

"You can map the interior layout of their ship from here?"

She opened her eyes. "How do you think we fold between the surfaces of worlds light-years apart? I'm ready. Enable the timer and set it for ninety seconds."

"You have got to be fucking kidding..."

"Our time is short," she said again, and I set the timer.

Moments later the raider touched the bomb and then both she and the bomb disappeared.

Forty-five seconds after that the raider returned, without the bomb.

"I think I have given it good placement to make sure the planet killing drone is thoroughly destroyed. The carrier ship will be very heavily damaged, but I'm uncertain whether its fold drive will be completely disabled. These are very massive and solid objects."

"You're sure they didn't detect your folding?"

"We know the limits of their processes very exactly, having made the components ourselves. Nanite based fold drives cannot detect our activity at all."

Moments later, the raider said "The bomb has gone off. It has seriously disrupted them."

"I don't see anything," I said.

"It will take about twelve minutes for the light to reach us here," M said.

While we were waiting, the raider said "There is still fold activity. They are trying to execute a detuned fold. They aren't close enough to anything for it to couple with reliably but they are trying different configurations. We need to finish destroying them."

She put coordinates into our fold drive again. "Fold in to here, about half a million kilometers range. Their damaged drive won't be able to detect yours at that range and we will be able to see and gauge the extent of destruction."

M folded us in. We folded inward past the shell of radiation and blinding light and were still well outward of the larger ejected wreckage. The Rate of Change had been built in the form of a regular octahedron with rounded vertices, and each facet had a large moveable mirror mounted at its center. Through the telescope we could see that one of its corners had been blown completely off, and what was inside was glowing ominously.

"Those big mirrors are their sunlight cannons," the raider said. "If we fold over to face the destroyed vertex at close range they won't be able to target us and we will be able to target the deep interior of the ship."

"Won't there be a lot of debris? There's only a quarter inch of aluminum between us and the vacuum of space."

"As with the light and radiation, hopefully we will fold past all that."

"Hopefully?"

"This is war," M said, and she used the sunlight RCS to exactly match velocity and orient us then executed the fold.

We all donned welding goggles and strapped in in case the gravity plating should fail. The interior of the fold ship was a seething mass of molten structural material, but the center had been somewhat shielded by the mass of the ship. "I'm drilling it," M said, and she opened up the cannon.

"They have redoubled their efforts at fold configurations. At this close range even their damaged drive can detect what we are up to," the raider Curator said. "They are trying to target us." We became aware of bits of debris flashing to incandescence around us and dinging our hull, but we were well in the shadow of the ship to all their functional cannons. Our ship was also buffeted by gas and debris from the hole M was drilling, but she used the RCS to hold us steady.

After about two minutes there was a flare from inside the fold ship. "Fold activity has ceased," the raider said. "I suggest retreat." We folded back to our observation position and watched. Finally the raider nodded. "Their fold drive is dead. If any of them remain alive they won't be for long."

That was the first point in the encounter when it occurred to me that we had just killed a few thousand sapient beings. People like us in many ways. But I knew M would remind me that they were enemies that were trying to kill us too, in spectacularly genocidal fashion.

"How sure are we?" M asked. "We've gone through too much here to let them slip away."

"As far as my instruments can tell their sunlight cannons should also be dead."

M folded back and resumed drilling. She didn't stop until the entire fold ship split into three pieces, forced apart by the pressure of boiling gases from within. "I can now verify that their fold drive is fully destroyed," the raider said."

"Okay. Thanks for the help."

"No need for that, we Curators bear..."

"Oh shit."

"What?"

"We've taken damage. We're leaking air and fuel cell oxygen and I'm not sure about the control surfaces and propellers." We all went back into the cargo area, which had windows. The wings were pockmarked with dents and tears and two of the four propellers were missing at least one blade. "We're in bad shape," M announced. "I don't think I can get it to the surface of a planet like this. We might not even make it through the velocity adjustment at Neptune with these leaks."

"There is no need," the Curator said. "Can you execute one more fold to get us just a bit closer to Kattegat?"

"The fold drive is one thing that does still seem to be working for now."

A few minutes later we held hands and closed our eyes, and when we opened them we were safe in front of the Earth embassy on Kattegat as our faithful ship Mail Service burned up crashing into one of its seas.

Episode 19

We rushed to the door of the embassy and knocked, fortunately getting their attention and gaining entrance before anyone outside noticed us. There were only a few embassy personnel present at that time, but M knew two of them personally and they expressed shock at our arrival because they were certain they knew of every human on Kattegat.

We hustled off to the embassy's most private communications room and arranged a hasty microfold call to Earth. There M, the raider-form Curator, and I each told our stories four times to successively higher level officials; our audience for the last retelling included the President of the United States and the highest leaders of several of our allies.

"What do the Curators recommend?" the Director asked of our Curator, without mentioning that one of the humans on his end was actually also a Curator.

"The raiders are a proud people who will be strongly tempted to react in kind. We have been inclined to forgive what they did in their attack on you, because it was unintended and the result of your surprise show of force, and they seem to be as horrified as everyone else and have directed their space captains to make sure it never happens again. But the possibility of this escalating is strong and we must not allow that."

"We will have the same problem here on Earth," someone who sounded an awful lot like the President said.

"The number of people who know about this is still very limited. Keeping a lid on it should still be possible."

"We still have to deal with the Sevillians."

"The Sevillians are our children and we reserve the right to discipline them in our own way. We need to find out how deep this rot goes into their culture. It is wasteful to fell the tree if only one branch is diseased."

"We need assurance that the problem is completely contained."

"I believe we can achieve that," came a voice from Earth we recognized as our human-form Curator. "We should chat a bit offline before finalizing decisions."

That seemed to inspire general agreement. After we ended the call, the raider-form Curator reminded us, "You two are still rock stars here. Everyone will go crazy if they find out you have returned, and thats even without considering that you just saved their world. We should depart as soon as possible."

"Our fold ship Edge of Space is on the roof of the power station and scheduled to return to Earth this afternoon. If we could quietly get M and J to the ship they could just take a stateroom and be on Earth within a day."

"I can get them there discreetly," the raider said. She offered us her hands, and moments later we were on the ship.

Edge of Space was a converted Boeing 747 and the captain showed us to a well-appointed room where we could safely hide from everyone else who was scheduled to fly with us. That gave us a chance to grab some sleep and some more entertaining not-sleep before touching down at JFK. Our human-form

Curator was there to meet us, and after we ducked into a hidden corner of the airport he folded us over to the fold project base.

If the rest of Earth and Kattegat were blissfully unaware of our brushes with genocide, the base was a beehive of activity. We had folded into the area where the fold inhibitor and span limiter had been built, and technicians were swarming over the inhibitor. "What the hell is going on?" M asked.

"We have engaged in one of your human rituals and made a purchase from you. We have offered a price for which to buy your fold inhibitor. We got a good deal because we had basically told you we wouldn't let you use it yourselves anyway."

"And what did you pay us for it?"

"Full technical theory of the operation of gravity plating. We offer a guarantee that you will be able to manufacture your own with your known existing manufacturing techniques and no use of nanites."

"That sounds fair," M said.

"Indeed, we expect it will lead you to a few more things. Meanwhile we have an immediate use for the inhibitor and no time to build our own."

"Seville?"

"Yes. Our agents there report that the general public has no knowledge of what was done in their name. Action must be taken but we hope that genocidal methods can be avoided this time. Here, we need to clear a space." At his direction everyone backed away from an area of the floor and a machine folded into it. It wasn't very big, and had the kind of gleaming perfect construction one might expect from molecular nanoassembly. Two aliens of different semi-humanoid species stepped out of it and one of them presented our Curator with what looked like a metal-link belt. Both of them sported the Mark of the Curators prominently, one on its forehead and the other on its lower back.

"More of our agents," our Curator said. "These are machines we use when we are terraforming and need to fold large apertures or work from uninhabitable spaces."

The new aliens took some measurements of the span limiter, and spoke with our Curator in alien tongue for a few moments. Then they got in their space pod and folded out.

"They will be arranging an operating environment and power supply for it," our Curator said.

"On Seville?"

"No, that would be too vulnerable. Deep below the surface of Seville's moon."

I thought of the effort that had been necessary for humans to reach our own Moon without the fold drive. With the inhibitor operating the Sevillians would be cut off from the rest of the galaxy and incapable of reaching the thing that was cutting them off. I almost felt sorry for them for a moment.

"So what's the belt for?" I asked innocently.

"It's an amplifier for our personal fold drives, which are normally tuned for an aperture the size of our bodies. I can fold my own body about a hundred light-years and cancel the likely velocity differences I'd find at that range with my implanted drive. But if I hold your hands and include you in the aperture, my range drops to a light-year or so and my ability to cancel velocity drops too. I would not be able to get your fold inhibitor to your own Moon on my own, much less to Seville's. But with this, I can fold an asteroid half-way across the galaxy, or an entire rocky planet a good distance across its solar system. These are the tools we use to explore and create new inhabitable worlds."

"That sounds insanely dangerous," I said.

"Only Curators with implanted drives can use these tools, and only when properly unlocked. We restrict access to those who have a need for them. I will be returning this when we have taken care of the current situation."

"You keep these on your homeworld?" M asked.

At this the Curator hesitated. "No," he said with a hint of emotion. "Our homeworld was destroyed aeons ago when our home star, which was much like your Sol, entered the next phase of its stellar evolution and became a red giant."

"Surely you could have saved it?"

"That was considered," he said heavily. "But if we moved it to a new orbit it would no longer be harmonically tuned to our system's other worlds. Our leaders then realized that there are some things in the cosmos that simply end. By that time we were quite capable of walking among our children undetected and we decided to move into the garden we'd spent so much effort to create. We have caches all over the galaxy of tools we might need once in awhile, and of course we continue to do what we have always done and create new inhabitable worlds."

"Do you remember your homeworld?"

"Oh no. We can live a very long time; I personally met one of the team who arranged your Earth's K-T impactor event. But Home was swallowed by our sun more than four billion of your years ago. It's not that we remember our home, but that we don't really have one at all now."

"You met someone who helped wipe out the dinosaurs? Is he still on Earth?"

"Oh no, he was part of the long-term evolution team. They were the ones who decided life had settled into an unuseful equilibrium and made the decision to disrupt it. Once it became clear that one of your ancestral species was likely to enter the critical path, they all moved out for other projects. I was part of the new team to foster critical path development. More experts came in as your ancestors approached, entered, and ascended the path. And of course there are other teams that specialize in early solar-system engineering to make stable orbits and stabilizing moons for habitable worlds, and then for seeding and nurturing early life."

"When did you come to Earth?"

"Relatively recently, about three hundred thousand years ago. But humans are my fifth professional project. You're going to make a mark on my resume, too."

I was about to say something when two of M's pilot friends recognized her and hailed us. "So you two slew the deadly fold ship again," one of them said.

"Getting to be a bad habit," M said modestly.

"Well we took care of the one here. Even brought our ship back in one piece. Good thing too since it was Grasshopper."

"You two flew my ship?"

"It's the only one with both the sunlight cannon and the new manually adjustable aperture fold drive."

"I thought we were going to nuke them."

"After you left some of the bigwigs got cold feet about that. We reviewed what you guys did to the raiders, and decided to try drilling it with the sunlight cannon instead. When it stopped retrying the bad fold we enveloped it and folded it into a collision course with Venus."

"Venus?" I said. "Why not the Sun or the Moon?"

"Moon's too accessible," the other pilot said nonchalantly. "Didn't want anyone trying to pick up the pieces and put it back together. Sun would have taken too long, a month or more to fall in depending on how close we dared folding in to leave it. With Venus we could fold into the planet's nighttime shadow, RCS away from the enemy drone, fold just ourselves out, and an hour later whatever's left of it after impact is melting on the surface."

"Smooth," M said.

"And we brought your ship back in one piece," the first pilot repeated.

"Well your target didn't have two fold drives and wasn't shooting at you."

A little while later one of the human technicians approached us. "I was told to tell you when we were ready, sir," he said to the Curator.

"Is the away installation team ready to depart?"

"Yes, sir."

"Have them stand on top of the inhibitor with all the parts and tools they will need for the installation as if we are preparing for a group photo. I'll join you shortly." He turned to us. "I'd like the two of you to come with us if you can," he said. "There are truths that must be penetrated at Seville before we activate this machine, and your presence would probably help."

The inhibitor itself was about three meters high and ten meters across. We all climbed the stairs and stood atop it. Our

Curator looked at his belt with a hint of a smile and raised his arms.

Then the whole machine and all of us were in a new space much more brightly and evenly lit and we were a lot less heavy. We, the machine, and the whole crew and their tools had folded to a new world without falling toward an attractor to adjust velocity, without using a RCS to adjust our orientation, and without doing any course corrections. We were in a freshly made cavern with life support and power on Seville's moon, over eighty light-years from Earth, and we had folded in with a large machine to make perfect contact with the floor in one seamless step.

Episode 20

The technicians fanned out to begin their tasks with quiet confidence; they weren't being shot at and they had a well-defined job to complete. There were other aliens present of varous form, all of whom turned out to actually be Curators, who assisted and began suggesting modifications, which the technicians carefully considered.

"The inhibitor itself is basic silicon substrate and by design redundant," our human-form Curator told us. "But your power supplies use some components which might not have the longevity we seek. Fortunately we have the technology at hand to bypass those and power the silicon directly."

"Where's the power coming from?"

"Photovoltaic nanite network on the surface with a storage layer for the lunar night. It's still knitting out but should be done before nightfall, and it's already adequate for direct power in the day."

Unlike the technicians who were nodding and pointing to connection points, M and I had no real idea why we were there. New Curators of different form popped in and out from time to time and after an hour or so a Sevillian appeared.

"Also one of ours," our Curator said before we could ask. "Greetings old friend *scree*."

THE CURATORS

"And yourself. I haven't seen you since you helped us get these guys through the path."

"You worked on the Seville project?" M asked our Curator.

"Oh yes. In that day I walked among them as *scree* here does now. Quite a different experience."

"Senses are senses," the Sevillian form Curator said. "And in this case, senseless is senseless."

"It is also a pun in Sevillian," our Curator said to M and me. "So what's it like down there?"

"Nobody knows about it. The xenocide project has been kept under a tight lid of secrecy by those who moved it forward. Many of the acts they performed to get it done were obviously criminal under Sevillian law. The resources they diverted to create the death drones have already created an economic recession and many people have been trying to figure out why it's happening."

"Well they're about to find out."

"Maybe what we're doing here is a little harsh," I suggested.

"We have discussed this at our highest levels all across the galaxy," the Sevillian said. "An example must be made."

"Do they have any assets off-system?"

"Not many, both of their remaining fold ships are in orbit now. They have a few individuals on other worlds but not enough to establish a stable colony, should anyone even let them try."

We consulted with the technicians. The conversion and installation was almost complete. The human built power supplies and control panel had been completely bypassed; the inhibitor would be activated by a timer of Curator design.

"Are all our people off-world?"

"Actually a lot of them have elected to stay. We have made sure they understand there will be no back door past the inhibitor, but this is also galactic history being made and they want to bear witness. And the expected blackout duration isn't that long for us."

"How long are you going to shut them out?"

"Long enough to make an impression. Their grand council is in session. I think it's about time to crash it. Humans, if you don't mind?" He extended his hands, and M and I each took one. Moments later we were in an auditorium full of Sevillians obviously engaged in the business of state. M and I were hearing translation even though we weren't wearing obvious translation hardware.

"What is the meaning of this?" one Sevillian shouted. "Who are these aliens and how have they appeared in our chamber?"

"We have come to judge you," the Sevillian Curator said and while the translation was calm the original sounds it was making boomed through the chamber.

"Guards!"

"The doors won't open!"

Six Sevillians advanced on us with weapons drawn. Our Curators looked at one another and waved their arms, and the weapons dissolved into dust.

"I did not know you could do that," I muttered.

"We couldn't do it to *you*," our human-form Curator muttered back. "But you know how your people have been wondering if we put back doors into the nanite technology? Now you know."

One of the representatives slowly approached us as everyone else was backing away, and I realized it was my original contact K, who had once made an appointment with a well-known but not very space savvy human dermatologist. "Not possible," K said. "What manner of trickery is this. Are you human J?"

"Yes," I said, as the chamber went quiet. It was a riot of color as the representatives reacted to the situation and their dermis announced their feelings.

"YOU ARE DEAD!" K shouted. It looked at M. "And you! And you! HOW ARE YOU HERE?"

"That is what we are here to explain. How many of your colleagues know of these?" Above our heads a holographic display appeared of the two death drones at station. There was much muttering in the chamber.

"You know what they are," I said to K.

"Of course I do," it spat. "You excreted on the equilibrium of our galaxy. You rewarded our enemies with powerful technology and brought them to our door. You are spreading through the unclaimed worlds of our galaxy like vermin. We did what was necessary."

"What did you do?" several voices said from the gallery.

"We exterminated the vermin," K said. "These will be among the last of their kind. As it should be."

"They made a realization they thought was quite clever, but like almost everything it's not as new as they thought," the Curator said. "A fold drive whose *only* purpose is to detune and fold a planet into its star does not need to be manned to perfect its calibration. So they built two dedicated planet-killing drones, and sent one to Earth and the other to Kattegat, the homeworld of those you call the raiders."

"And how did they fund this murderous extravagance?"

"You will probably find that much of it was illegal, and has caused your current economic downturn."

"It doesn't matter," K spat. "We did what had to be done."

"And you failed," M said. "Our team stopped you at Earth, and J and I ambushed your ship Rate of Change and destroyed it before it could deliver the other drone to Kattegat."

"Lies! We have the sunlight cannon now." At this a gasp went up from the chamber. "Your ships have hulls of gossamer, how could you possibly prevail against one of our capital ships?"

"We didn't use the sunlight cannon. We used a hydrogen bomb." The Curators helpfully put up a projected image of the Rate of Change with its blown-off apex and the ominous glow from within. Another gasp from the chamber.

"YOU ARE ABOMINATIONS!" K shouted, and several Sevillians came forward to restrain it before it could attack us.

"We created you," the Sevillian-form Curator said to the chamber. "We formed your world from the cosmic dust, gave it a moon and the right conditions for life to thrive. We seeded your world with life and we guided it, forming your tree of life and your genus and your ancestral species. We gave you encouragement to evolve intelligence and in time language and writing and science and technology. We gave you nanites and the fold drive. And you have thanked us for our gifts by using them to try to murder our other children."

There was a ripple in the chamber as someone with obvious authority descended from the audience to the dais. "Your power is obvious," it said. "Most of us did not know of this transgression which was done in our name. What are your intentions?"

"The last time this happened was over a billion years ago," the Sevillian-form Curator said. "In that case it started a planet-folding war. We had to end it by folding twenty worlds into their stars ourselves, to fully cure the disease."

"We will do whatever we can to atone."

"You have the humans to thank for the fact that you are still alive. They have given us a new option. There will be hardship, but your kind will have a second chance."

"I know my people will ask why we are being punished, but not those of Kattegat who did fold one of your worlds into its sun."

"That was the act of a desperate crew who were surprised by an existential threat they did not expect. And the world they folded did not harbor a critical path species or post critical path civilization. Their leaders were horrified to learn of what happened and quickly instructed their space captains to make sure it must never happen again. And the humans exercised mercy, and without our encouragement decided to rectify the problem by solving the problem that made the raiders become raiders in the first place, their starvation for raw materials, rather than exacting revenge. Meanwhile, even though you had never even been attacked your leaders devoted significant resources to the purpose of xenocide. They had not been surprised and knew just what they were doing."

"In that case, we gratefully accept your decision to grant us a second chance. May I ask just what our hardship will be, and for how long?"

"You will find out its form soon enough. As for the duration, we will see if a thousand of your years gives you time to reflect on what was done in your name."

As M and I were still sucking in our breath our Curator grabbed our hands and suddenly we were back on Seville's moon, where all the human technicians and aliens were gone. The Curator activated a control panel and motioned for our hands again, saying "Quickly!" Moments later we were on a transparent glass surface elevated far above a desert landscape.

"My mother brought me here when I was a child," M said. "The Grand Canyon Skywalk, isn't it?"

"Yes. My people have a saying that when you have to do something ugly, you should remind yourself of something beautiful. Your people made this bridge purely for the purpose of celebrating the beauty of the world we gave you. This would have been lost if the Sevillians had succeeded in their plan."

"It was just a few of them," I said.

"It only takes a few, and a lot more supporting and following them blindly, as your people learned over time. It's a terrible thing that it happened, but your people know genocide. The Sevillians don't. They are still able to think of it as a cleansing process. But as violent as humans can be, you have also learned the hard way just how much so much blood costs. You applied the same lesson to the raiders that you have applied to your own nations in recent time and we are quite proud of you."

We watched as the Sun sank toward the horizon. "How do we know the Sevillians will learn the same thing from their millenium of exile?"

"Oh we don't," he said as the twilight deepened. "But if they don't, there is always still plan A."

Episode 21

Four Years Later

It had been six months with M working on some super-secret project she couldn't even talk to me about, and me doing diplomatic missions. I'd learned to fly, and even though it wasn't official and I should have had no business going near an airplane much less a starship the Director had decided on his own authority that my skills were sufficient to take control of a machine that cost tens of millions of dollars to build and guide it to the stars.

The flying part was a little easier for me because when you're coming in from space you can pick a landing spot that has good weather and daylight. Still, not all of the alien airstrips are up to human standards so some care is necessary. But my function was mostly diplomatic and commercial. Humans weren't selling our number one product, the miniature fold drive, to other races yet because it still cost us over ten million dollars to build one of them and we were absorbing our own entire production of one every month or two. But we were using the ships we built to provide a service lots of races were willing to pay for—next day delivery.

For aeons the rule was that interstellar travel took about a month. The actual journey for the foldship only took a day or two, but because the ships were so large and couldn't land loading and unloading them from orbit could take weeks. It was an enormous logistical nightmare that nobody had ever really solved. But then along come humans, who for a price can be there in less than a day, pick up your load whether it be emergency disaster relief or guests for a royal wedding, and have you to your destination in just a few more hours. We had far more requests for business than we had ships to provide service, and about forty human employees just working on appropriate methods of payment that we could usefully accept. Most of the galaxy didn't use money, and we had to establish products and raw materials that made sense as barter. We also had people working on what we were pretty sure would become a galactic bank because the barter thing was becoming such a pain in the ass.

But now M was done with her secret mission and we had some time together. When I met her I saw that our friendly human-form Curator was already there too. "You said you had something really special to show me," I teased. "I thought it would involve less clothes."

"Later for that. We can always boink, but you don't always see the first of a new generation of starship."

M led us out behind the hangar where a really strange craft was parked. It had three somewhat normal-looking aircraft hulls linked by connecting tunnels and struts, and it was sitting on pylons instead of wheeled landing gear.

"The good ship Trinity," M said by way of introduction.

"I thought you were an atheist," the Curator said.

"She's named after the character from **The Matrix**."

"So our next-level interstellar craft is a trimaran?" I teased.

THE CURATORS

M laughed. "You should be so glad you weren't involved with those discussions. We're obviously still using a lot of aircraft parts because they are readily available, but Trinity was never an airplane. Cylinders are still the second-best shape for a pressure containment vessel that has to maintain atmospheric pressure in space. We could have used a single bigger one, but that would have been more vulnerable; Trinity's three hulls can be isolated from one another. We have been in shooting wars, remember. All four connecting tunnels can be isolated and used as airlocks. Her primary piloting station is in the center hull with the large transparent forward hemisphere, but she can be piloted from anywhere by wire and the safety glass windows in the side hulls are much stronger than the primary cockpit transparent dome. She's a prototype, and in this form her left hull is configured for passenger service and her right hull for cargo with a C130 style rear cargo door. The middle hull is propulsion, engineering, and logistics."

"How does she get to the ground without wings?" I asked.

The Curator smiled as M answered. "You know, our biggest surprise at getting our payment for the Seville fold inhibitor is that gravity plating is yet another fold application. It's like the microfold we use for communication and the sunlight cannon and power reactor, but it is even more restrictive and only passes gravitons. We had no proof gravitons even existed and now we're using them."

"I thought it would take a particle accelerator the size of a solar system to detect them," I said.

"It did," the Curator said.

"So gravity plating scarfs up gravitons from all sources through a really detuned microfold, as does levitation plating which is gravity plating turned upside down and backward which is what powers the flying cars. But we realized that we could use the same principle in a tuned fashion, since we're making our own fold hardware. So we can make a gravity microfold to some place with really usefully intense gravity flux, like a neutron star. Trinity doesn't have to fold out to Neptune and fall to adjust its velocity. It can fold Neptune's gravity to wherever it is. And even better it can fold the gravity of the Sun or a neutron star or black hole to wherever it is. Trinity can accelerate at over a hundred gravities. Once we have the controls perfected it should be able to take off from Earth, match velocity with Kattegat, fold over and land in about an hour."

"That sounds a bit dangerous," I said.

"Actually it isn't," the Curator said. "We once made ships similar to this. Since the gravity field affects all particles of the ship equally, there are no tidal forces or internal acceleration. Should the drive fail the ship would simply stop accelerating; there is no hazard of mismatched correction. And the graviton microfold doesn't pass any of the other extreme environmental hazards."

"Have you done any of this stuff yet?"

"Space trials only," M said. "I wanted to offer both of you the chance to be with me for the first real journey."

"I accept gratefully," the Curator said.

"And I guess I do too."

Because it was on relatively short shock-absorbing pylons instead of tall landing gear, Trinity's connecting tunnel hatches folded down into staircases that neatly met the ground. "Where are we going?" I asked as M fired up the ship's systems.

"I was going to ask for suggestions."

"I do have one," the Curator said. "Do you have pressure suits on board?"

"Of course."

"I have been asked to do an errand which would normally involve bothering those Curators who are keepers of our powerful technology. But if this ship can land on an airless world, we could let them sleep."

"Well, that sounds like a good idea. Let's start by landing on a closer airless world." We sat in the jump seats behind M in the center fuselage piloting station. Trinity arose silently from the surface of the Earth, then tilted upward and shot forward vertically for a few minutes until we were in the blackness of space. No fold maneuvers were necessary to divest ourselves of Earth's air. When we were well into space M folded us out to Earth's Moon.

At the Moon we adjusted velocity in seconds and descended, until we were looking at the descent stage and flag of an Apollo mission. "I'm not going to actually touch down and desecrate this place. I wouldn't have come here at all if I had to use thrusters to descend. But this is the landing place of Apollo 17. We are the first people to see it with our own eyes since Cernan and Schmitt left here in 1972."

"This is a great honor," our Curator said, and I think he meant it.

"Where do we go from here?" I asked.

"If I may," the Curator said. "There is an outer world in the Seville system where I have a chore to do. It is well outside of the reach of your fold inhibitor, which is why it is there."

M folded us off to the Seville system. At the Curator's directive she homed in on a spot on its fourth rocky planet, a frozen wasteland similar to Ceres. There was a modest sized machine on the surface with a small array of stick antennas. After we touched down the Curator suited up, went out to the device, and touched it with an object he had brought with him. Minutes later he was back in the ship.

"That's our back channel relay," he said after unsuiting. "The natives have no knowledge of it, it's entirely for the use of our stay-behind Curators. But they had been getting some interference from local radio transmissions. We had quite forgotten to give our people the ability to reprogram its frequency profile remotely, since we're kind of used to being able to get to these things in person. The program update I just performed fixes that for them."

"You've been getting updates from Seville? What the hell has been happening there?"

"Let's go somewhere that serves alcohol to discuss that. My agents have told me of an excellent pub on Kattegat, and I hear the two of you have no need to pay for drinks on that world."

Of course the space traffic directors at Kattegat expected us to need the roof of the power station for a rolling landing, and they were surprised when we asked for a courtyard of modest dimensions in the city near a certain trendy address. This was quickly arranged, and it was indeed about an hour after the Curator updated his relay that we touched down in a small vacant lot between two very Earthlike wooden buildings. We walked around a few corners and found the pub.

Over large glasses of rich fermented beverage, the Curator told us what had happened after the inhibitor went online. "Nearly all of the power failed, of course," he said. "We get used to using the fold drop repeaters because, like hydroelectric, they work all the time. But nanites can also make good photovoltaic and supercapacitor power storage stations. The Sevillians knew their hardship was a punishment and did not waste time lamenting it. They set about dismantling their now useless fold drop repeaters and building solar fields and batteries. Most of the planet was without power for less than a year, and they managed to save that year's agricultural crops so there was no famine."

"I'm glad that there wasn't a lot of death," I said.

"Well the crews of the two orbiting foldships had no way home; as you now know the repulsor plating is fold based. They said their goodbyes via radio and opened the airlocks. And the leaders who had created the xenocide program were publicly tried and put to death. The Sevillians had not imposed the death penalty for thousands of years but they found this particular crime a bit over the top. And of course there were the minor tragedies you would expect as people found themselves in flying transports that could no longer fly and similar situations. Still it was a very small percentage of their global population."

"Do you know what happened to K?"

"Not specifically, but I would be very surprised if it was not put to death with the rest of the would-be xenocides. Our repeater doesn't have a lot of bandwidth. It only functions at all about thirty percent of the time due to astrophysical alignments, and manages about ten bits per second best case when it does. We're limited because our ground agents are pretending to be amateur radio operators, and don't have proper radio telescope dishes. So we mostly get what amount to newspaper clippings."

"So what are things like now, four years later?" M asked.

"Sevillian civilization has mostly recovered from the insult. They were a self-sufficient world before we gave them the fold and they are self-sufficient again now without it. You may recall the elder gentlebeing who came down from the balcony to challenge us; it was their supreme leader many years ago and after we folded out it was reappointed by acclimation. It led the trials of the xenocides and the organization of replacement networks for the infrastructure disabled by the fold inhibitor. It also kept up awareness that a great wrong had been attempted in their name, for which they all had responsibility. The result has been similar to the situation in your country of Germany after the unpleasantness of your second World War. There is a subpopulation of die hards who would kill anything that disagrees with them on general principle, but they are a small minority and not generally tolerated. The official and popular view is that they were betrayed by leaders who misled them and attempted to make them all agents of murder, and that this cannot ever be tolerated. It will be interesting to see how well this attitude persists across future generations."

"I still think we are maybe being a bit too harsh making them live with it for a thousand years."

"Well it's done," the Curator said. "How would you propose to disable it? It's deep beneath the surface of an airless world shielded by the inhibitor itself. If you get within two astronomical units of it your ship becomes a flying brick."

"Right."

We talked a bit more then made our way back to the ship, which was now surrounded by a small crowd of local raiders. At our approach there was a collective "Ooooooh" and as we

THE CURATORS

opened the hatch one of the kittens said, "How did you get it here?"

"You'll see very soon," M said mischievously.

"Thanks for saving our world," he added. The secret hadn't lasted long. Fortunately none of them recognized us as individuals.

"Just promise us that if you're ever in the position to do it for another people, you'll do the same yourselves."

At that the crowd did their stomping salute, and we stomped back as we'd learned to do on our first visit. Then we closed the hatch and lifted off in perfect silence while they gaped, and in less than an hour we were back on Earth eating dinner.

Episode 22

B*egin Article*
For Immediate Release via Microfold Relay
Scope: All-Galaxy
Section: Lifestyle and Customs
Origin: Sagittarius R22 Lee 6 Curator Index:807422
Translation Note: Names with no recorded Earth equivalents are given Greek placeholders according to current Earth [CI:1742660] directive.
Title: At an Ancient Ritual, a New Ship Gets the Party Together
Byline: Alpha and Beta

Galactic rotation may have carried the ancient civilization of Gamma [CI:407914] out of the mainline of the Sagittarius arm of our galaxy, but their traditions still require personal attendance of their allies at the ascendance rituals of their royalty. The last time these reporters covered a Gamma royal event it took more than half a typical lunar month to pick up all the guests, and a similar interval to get them all back home, despite Gamma reserving a capital fold ship for the purpose.

This time they did it in one typical solar day each way. And what made it possible was a remarkable new ship built by the humans of Earth [CI:1742660].

THE CURATORS

Humans are as young a species as the Gammas are mature; they only left critical path quarantine within the last few hundred years. But they are burning a bright line along their arm of the Galaxy. After building an improbably compact fold drive they created a lot of buzz with their tiny starships, all of which had originally been built for on-planet air transport before being retrofitted for space. And while those ships could manage the stunning feat of ascent to space, folding, velocity translation, and descent to the surface all in one trip, that trip was described as either thrilling or terrifying depending on who you asked. Those craft got to the surface with loud air-breathing combustion engines full of moving parts subjected to high temperatures and unimaginable stresses, and while our Beta did take the trip between worlds on one, at that time they didn't even have gravity plating and so it was a bit of a wild ride.

That was five typical years ago—and, well, for humans it seems five years is a heck of a long time.

[Photo: Human-M-Hatchway] *Our pilot M welcomes us to the journey.*

We caught the new bus at Gamma, joining princess Delta to collect her guests. The human foldship *Three-In-One* features not just gravity plating but a supergravity drive capable of accelerating it at the surface gravity of whatever cosmic object, usually the nearest star, it decides to tap. It's a much more focused version of our gravity and levitation plating, which we can't make with nanites. The humans are quite open about how they make their unusual technology, and so far nobody else has been inclined to duplicate the heroic manufacturing effort it takes.

One might at first mistake the Three-In-One for a ground to orbit transport, but its human pilot M joked that the ship has actually never been in orbit around a planet. "We just don't need to do that," she said as we toured the small ship which has no staterooms and comfortable but close seating for about a hundred standard form bipedal beings in its passenger hull. "We pop from the surface to near space, make the fold, adjust velocity if necessary, and touch down. Tapping the surface gravity of a nearby normal star gives us twenty plus normal habitable gravities of acceleration for the velocity adjustment, and we can orient the vector in any direction without turning the ship. We can be surface to surface within galactic distances like this in half an hour."

[Photo: Human-J-Attending] *Human J provides treats to the passengers.*

While they weren't providing the usual palacious staterooms, the humans did put on a good spread of alcoholic liquors and savory snacks. While they had a few traditional exotica known to be favored by certain guests most of the treats were from Earth, and offered an interesting sample of their brewing, distilling, agricultural, and meat cultivating skills. It also became a bit of a running gag among those of us who had experienced a Three-In-One transport cycle to rib the newcomers who hadn't about how terrible the accommodations were, until they saw for themselves how quickly the whole thing was going to be accomplished.

After an incredible run of visiting eight worlds in less than half a typical day, we returned to Gamma with all the guests, landing and delivering them directly within the main courtyard of the royal palace. There was no rest for our transport

THE CURATORS

hosts though; during the festival the Three-In-One would go back to Earth and do a transport run through their colonies and a diplomatic run to their allies at Kattegat on the far side of the galaxy before returning to take all the guests home.

The leaders of eight worlds have much to contemplate after this improbably quick ride. Humans have done things in their short years of maturity which the rest of us haven't managed in aeons, a fact that hasn't gone lost on some of our leaders—including, unfortunately, those of the world Seville [CI:1729140] which earned a Curator-imposed exile by attempting to destroy both Earth and their allied world Kattegat [CI:1659441] with the very fold drive shenanegans they scare us with as kids.

We suppose the lesson from what happened there is, don't do it. You can't stop change by murder. And why would you want to, when that change holds so much wonderful promise?

The human ship Three-In-One has only been in operation for about four typical lunar months. Its operators say it is really a prototype, a conservative expression of designs they know will work without venturing too far out in the realm of what is unknown but possible.

We are looking very forward to seeing what the humans find out to be possible next.

Footnote:

Those who are unfamiliar with humans might wonder why our hosts are wrapped in so much textile decoration as they attend us. This was not some special affectation for our royal guests; in addition to their unusual technological talents, humans are known for a somewhat perverse modesty habit and instinct to conceal their natural body form. This can be most frustrating for the curious, but fortunately their allies at Kattegat tempted the female pilot M to accept and display color honors for her triumphant defeat of their own foldship. Here are M and J, M without her typical human modesty garments and sporting raider colors, along with exalted raider colorist O in a candid moment on the local planetary show When Not Raiding.

[Photo: Humans-Candid-With-Color]

End Article

The entire article was professionally matted and framed, including all three photos, in the hallway about twenty feet from the Director's office door.

"I seem to recall predicting that this would happen," I said carefully.

"So you did," M said.

"It doesn't bother you?"

"Do you have any idea what this really means?" M said.

"I guess I don't."

"Humans are about to become the most famous young race in the galaxy. Aliens by the trillion are going to remember Earth's Curator Index 1742660 and dream about piloting tiny starships that can land on planets. And they will all wonder what a human looks like. And over most of the galaxy, it will be *us*"—she stabbed the last photograph on the poster with her forefinger—"that they will see. Not our political leaders, not our rock stars, not our diplomats or our engineers. They will see the naked female who blows up fold ships and her faithful statesman mate who made the improbable peace."

And with that she kissed me and then turned and walked away, looking as self-satisfied as I have ever seen any human being in my entire life.

I realized as I detoured by the liquor store on the way back to our house that I should never underestimate the ego of a warrior test pilot.

Episode 23

The Director caught us as we were moving our stuff from Trinity to the Horse Pill to do a little scouting for new colony world candidates. Horse Pill looked exactly like what it was named after, a huge gel cap about seven meters long and three in diameter. It was a generous accommodation for a two-person scouting crew and our instruments, and much quieter and really less conspicuous than Grasshopper, which was being fitted to hang from the roof of the Smithsonian Air and Space museum.

Fold drives being a rather valuable commodity, Grasshopper's had found its way into the Horse Pill.

"You guys might want to make a detour," the Director said as he waved a tablet at us. "We've gotten a rather interesting message. An invitation from a new race, but directed specifically at you two. And they want you to visit rather than them coming here."

M scanned the tablet as I asked, "Are we sure it's legit?"

"Checks out with several other mature races on the CI. It's from their current royal leader, so it would be good diplomacy to pay our respects."

"On it," we said together as M handed the tablet back.

"They named their own world in English?" I asked as we loaded the Horse Pill.

"Yes, they call it Hyacinth. Isn't that an Earth flower?"

"This is going to be different."

We had Hyacinth's Curator Index and therefore its current location and other useful data. With the supergravity drive and such a small ship we were in contact with Hyacinth ground control within forty-five minutes.

"Wait a minute, is the controller speaking English? This isn't a translator?"

"No, not on our end and I don't think on theirs either."

Our approach took us in low over a large city. In the center of town was something I'd never seen on an alien world, a tall shaft-like building towering over the rest of the city. "That's impressive," I said as we approached.

"They want us to notice it," M said. "Our instructions are to land on its roof."

Before we dropped the hatch we could see our greeting party through the nose dome, a group of four bright blue feathered bipedal aliens. They had large curved beaks instead of lips, and their Mark of the Curators was a bow-tie of yellow feathers just below the collar. One of them wore some kind of decorative body harness.

We exited our craft and the leader with the harness offered a handshake. "Welcome to Hyacinth," he said in an oddly whistly version of English. "You may also refer to our race as the Hyacinth, and to myself as Ascendant Prince Henry."

"It must have taken some effort for you to learn our language," I said with what I hoped was a tone of respect. I couldn't figure out how he was speaking English without lips.

"And well worth it if it leads to the diplomatic result I hope for. Unless I am terribly mistaken I believe you are human pilot M, slayer of fold ships, and human diplomat J, tamer of raiders. It is an honor to welcome you to our world. If you would accompany us, I would like to show you a few things, and our technology for making a presentation isn't as portable as yours."

The elevator was typical alien tech, floating on repulsor plates to go up or down and locking in place with mechanical clips to access a destination floor. Earth elevator companies were already making plans to switch over and get rid of all the damn cables.

"How should we properly refer to you?"

"A proper question for a diplomat, human J. You can call me Prince Henry. We suggest you just use male pronouns to refer to all of us, since our genitalia are internal and we have neither primary nor secondary external sexual characteristics; most of our young people don't know what sex they are until they have a good reason to wonder."

"That must be... interesting. How *do* your people learn their sex?"

"Well, laying an egg is a major clue." This drew a clucking which we would learn was the Hyacinth natural form of laughter from the others. "Also being in a committed relationship with someone who lays a fertile egg is a clue. And for the impatient, there are always tomographic medical scans. But we really don't consider it that important unless we're actively trying to reproduce."

He motioned for us to take seats at a semicircular table facing a display screen. "So how do you like our building? I intend to make it the seat of our government once I ascend to the throne. As Ascendant Prince I am afforded much authority but not quite that much. With the notable exception of the wonders of your own Earth, we are fairly certain this is now the tallest building in the galaxy."

"I was told such structures were impossible with your nanite tech."

"And so they were until we learned a wonderful thing from you. This building is made of nanite matrix reinforced with glass fibers. We had to learn to make the fibers, since the nanites can't, and to teach the nanites to arrange and position them and then to bond to them as they built up matrix. We are still refining the technique but it is going to revolutionize a few things."

"How do you make the fibers?"

"We sent you several pallets of gravity plating in payment for basic machine tools and foundation hardware. Of course we could have just bought a fiberglass spinning machine, but we wanted the ability to make as many of our own as we might want, since we are thinking we might be wanting a lot of them before long."

"I've heard this 'we' from leaders before," I said a bit skeptically. "Do your people share this vision?"

"Why do you think I built this building?"

"What provoked such an interest in us? We've met dozens of species who mostly don't care what we've done, and one that got real pissed off about it."

"Unfortunate, that. A couple of years ago you provided transport for the royal guests to ... well, I can't pronounce that place's name either, but you'll remember it. Eight worlds in less than a day, in your ship Trinity. I was one of your passengers, and I was enthralled. Most people don't seem to care that they might be living in the midst of history being made, and others react like the Sevillians with terror. Maybe it's because I am young, but I see your emergence among us as an opportunity. I do not want to be the leader who let such an opportunity pass, and I want my people to benefit from the wonders that are likely to emerge."

"Your message indicated that you might have some particular wonder in mind."

"I do. But first, I have a couple of questions which concern your supergravity drive. I realize your fold drive is not for sale because you are using your own full production, and honestly I think that is the best use for those drives because none of us has the other arts ready to make such small and nimble ships. But I am hoping that the supergravity drive is simpler and that you might be willing to part with one or two of them for a suitable return. And I also need to know how far the supergravity field can be extended from the drive itself; I am hoping for at least a kilometer, preferably at least two."

I turned to M, since she's the technical expert. "On the first point we can make a lot more supergravity drives, because they don't need very accurate tuning to create a graviton flux. They are physically smaller and simpler and we complete them faster and get a better yield than we do with the fold drives. But we also have more use for them, since they form a basis for exploiting our solar system's extraterrestrial resources. We can use a supergravity-only ship for in-system exploration and transport. But the bottom line is that yes, we can make a lot more of them, so with a sufficient motive we could probably break a few loose for alternate purposes. On the second point, we've been locking them down since we don't want unsupervised people dragging asteroids around without authorization, but yes the field can be made several kilometers in radius."

Prince Henry nodded at one of his companions and an image appeared on the screen. "This is my vision," he said. "A nanite based fold ship. A bit on the small side by our standards, this concept vehicle has a pressure dodecahedron inscribing a sphere one point three kilometers in diameter. It also has an unpressurized skirt creating a ten-sided support pad with multiple gravity plated cargo levels. It is fiberglass reinforced, and therefore less than a third the mass of typical similar sized ships, an important feature because it has to be able to support its own weight in a gravity field. Because a supergravity drive will make it possible for this ship to land on the surface of a world."

The picture became animated and showed this, the ship touching down on a prepared landing area that would have to be a mile wide. "Loading and unloading such a ship would still be time consuming compared to what your small ships manage, but much faster and simpler than it would be via shuttles to orbit. And we could manage large population transfers and cargos that are far beyond your capacity."

M and I sucked in our breath at the same time. "That's an impressive vision," I said.

"And totally dependent on your help. It is absolutely unworkable without your supergravity drive, which we have proven cannot be duplicated with the nanites available to us. It will be thirteen Earth months before I ascend to the throne, but I can make plans. I want this to be the first great project of my reign."

"What would you be offering us for our supergravity drive?"

"I would actually be asking for more than just the drive. If the concept proves out, I will be building a coalition of worlds to make a manufacturing center to use your techniques to make supergravity drives for ourselves. I would ask for your help in that endeavour. You have said to others that you do not wish to hide your technology. We do not see any current added value in trying to duplicate your fold drive, but this is something for which I think we can make a case."

"That sounds reasonable, but you still haven't told us what's in it for us."

"We won't just build one prototype ship. We will build two." The image on the projector split so that it showed two landed mountain-sized foldships. "And in exchange for your help, we will give the second one to the humans of Earth to use as you wish."

Episode 24

By the time we visited Hyacinth and received an astonishing proposal from then-Prince Henry, the outline of an economic structure between Earth and the rest of the galaxy was beginning to become visible.

At the heart of this was the ultimate secret of gravity and repulsor plating. When we learned how to make these incredibly useful platings, we learned that by far the best and most effective way to make them was—with nanites. We could make plating with the techniques we used to make the fold and supergravity drives, but it didn't work any better and was more fragile and vastly more expensive.

Our leaders were still reluctant to delve into primary nanite manufacturing, both because of the danger of someone building a primitive and detunable nanite fold drive and because it was the lack of nanite tech that had forced us to explore other methods and develop our other unique capabilities. So we wrote up specifications and a catalog of possibly useful stuff we could provide that you couldn't easily make with nanites, and published them on the microfold network.

We had an insatiable appetite for repulsor plating because this was the motive force behind flying transport vehicles. It was strong enough to lift one of our small aircraft style starships, but not anything much heavier. It wasn't adequate for velocity adjustment after folding between regions of the galaxy. But it could power a flying car from a pack of AA batteries. And it was within the means of any interested alien community to follow our specifications for the tile types we wanted and make a steady supply of the stuff with sunlight for power and local minerals for raw materials.

In return we supplied commodity machines and tools; bearings, drill bits, extruded and threaded rods, nuts and bolts were all popular. It soon became common to find hybrid designs published on the microfold that were mostly made of nanites but also requiring precision parts from Earth. It didn't hurt that we could easily make delivery and take our trade items at the surface of other worlds. We offered discounts to worlds that could provide landing strips because we still had a lot more converted aircraft than Trinity style second generation ships, but we were building those as fast as we could.

The Bank of Earth was off to a solid start if only because the Earth industries that supplied our end of the trade wanted to be paid in money. And while it was new to them, the aliens who made a regular practice of dealing with us quickly realized that having funds in our bank gave them great flexibility when they were making wish lists from our catalog of available goods.

This was the situation when we brought the Hyacinth Regent of Technology Development to Reagan National Airport in the Horse Pill. He returned to Earth with us to give his presentation to a group of dignitaries and specialists for evaluation.

"Do we have some time before the meeting?" he asked as we landed. The Regent spoke excellent English as his Prince did, and instructed us to call him by the human name John.

"Yes, we were generous with the scheduling."

"If it's possible I would like to make a quick visit to your national zoo. I understand there is an underground transport that can take us there."

Fortunately it had become common enough for aliens to be seen on the streets of human cities, particularly capitals like Washington, that we didn't attract an unworkable amount of attention. At the zoo John skipped all the more spectacular exhibits and guided us straight to the tropical birds, where we found ourselves facing a pair of enormous bright blue parrots. The sign called them Hyacinth Macaws. Just like any tourist, John took a few pictures.

"Your named your world after them, not the flower?"

"Yes. The birds are themselves named after the flower, but these fellows are as closely related to us as anything on your world. Their coloration is nearly identical to ours. And while we have no flighted ancestors, like these birds our ancestors were ground-based feathered bipedal carnivores like many of your dinosaurs."

"And the Curators wiped out their dinosaur ancestors with an asteroid strike."

Regent John laughed, in his native Hyacinth way. "Yes, Curators will do that. Our ancestors tended to stubbornly get stuck in dead-end monster mode. They had to wipe out our ancestors three times before we came along."

Having seen the macaws we made our way back to the zoo entrance and then the subway. "Is there any significance to the human names you have chosen to take on?" M asked as we hiked down the hill toward the subway station.

"Prince Henry took the name of one of your own royalty he admires, Prince Henry the Navigator of Portugal. And for my anticipated role in our future development he suggested the name of John Frank Stevens, an engineer who is credited with making your ambitious Panama Canal project practical."

"Prince Henry knows an awful lot about our history," I said as we stepped onto the subway escalator.

"Prince Henry wants to learn from every available source. And most of what is out there has been known by everyone for billions of years. You humans are a fascinating exception."

Several hours later we were in the Oval Office. "This is not the meeting you came here for," the President said matter-of-factly. "But we want to know what this might mean before we present it to the rest of our world."

"It's a simple enough deal," John said. "We want a supergravity drive for our prototype, in return for a copy of our prototype surface landing fold ship. We assume you can outfit your ship with the supergravity and your own superior fold drive. And we would like your technical assistance setting up an independent manufacturing facility on a colony world which can make more supergravity drives."

"Before we could get any use out of this enormous ship we would have an incredibly difficult job outfitting it," one of the men in attendance said.

"How is that?" Regent John asked.

"This thing must have a hundred square kilometers of deck. It will need appointments, furniture, plumbing, lighting, and a thousand more details to make it useful. It would suck up a generation's resources and I'm not sure what we would do with it."

"Oh, I don't think you understand," the Regent said. "All those things are included. They are built-in by the nanite construction team. These ships have been made for aeons, and their construction has long been a well honed art. Despite the unique utility of being able to land, which will call for a few adjustments, most of the things you mention are long ago solved problems. We will deliver you a ship that is ready to board and fly once its drives are installed and calibrated."

"But what about toilets, food production and distribution..."

"Of course. Galaxy wide there are about twenty most common types of body form for hospitality purposes, differing in things like furniture size, bedding preferences, food supply and preparation and waste removal. Our usual practice is to outfit about half the ship as staterooms and the rest as functional gathering and work areas of different sizes, and to outfit about half the staterooms and work areas for the species that runs the ship with the others a varied mix. We have also studied your designs for things like toilets and sinks to tweak them to your preferred style. With nanites it's just a software problem."

"It would take a huge crew," the man said.

"It would, if you choose to use it that way. Most foldships have a large live-on crew. Then again, I understand most of your large seagoing vessels do too, and they can't fly between the stars."

The President spoke up. "Regent, would you like a tour of our historic White House? I need to have a word with my people."

"Of course. Do you allow photographs? My Prince will be fascinated."

"In most areas we do, the guide will let you know." He slapped the intercom and said "Theresa, we have an alien with the most beautiful blue feathers you've ever seen who needs a tour of our house."

After Regent John left the President eyed the man who had spoken up. "M and J, I don't think you've met my Secretary of Defense," he said.

"Actually I have sir," M said. "He gave me a medal once."

"What is your problem, H?" the President asked him.

"This is an enormous and unexpected undertaking," he said. "We have no budget for it, no schedule, no personnel, and it promises to dwarf important existing programs."

"H, stop thinking about blowing shit up for a change and think about what this means. Within the next twenty years they are telling me about five billion people are going to lose their homes due to sea level rise. They will need to go somewhere, but most of the somewhere they could go here on Earth is already occupied by other people who aren't going to want them. They will need to eat, and at least half our arable land is also going to go under or become desert. Maybe more. The very manufacturing facilities that our blue friend is so interested in are going to be flooded and destroyed by storms with ever increasing frequency. Have I left anything out? Am I blowing it out of proportion?"

"No, sir," he said quietly.

"This ship, this *one ship* could save our damn bacon. We have the colony worlds. The aliens have wondered why we planted flags on so many of them, that was thinking ahead. But we also have to get the people there and more importantly the infrastructure and industries to support them. It's been happening but it's *too slow*. M and J, would you say one of these ships could transport an entire city all at once, its buildings on those skirt decks and its population in the staterooms?"

"I'd say that's exactly what it's designed to do," M said.

"And Prince Henry is an avid student of our species," I added. "He may have anticipated this need and constructed an offer he knew we would be foolish to refuse."

"And we won't," the President said with finality. "We'll let Regent John present his offer, but the only question will be whether we tell them to paint a UN flag on the hull or a US flag. One way or the other we're giving them their damn gravity drive and we're *gratefully* taking the ship."

The next day the Regent made his case to the United Nations general assembly, and the President followed with his own. The vote wasn't even close; the ship would have a UN flag, and the deal would set a myriad of smaller preparatory plans in motion all across the Earth.

Episode 25

As the Laputa began construction in orbit at Hyacinth, the attention of our workgroup changed dramatically. Even assuming that the nanite construction teams delivered us a ready to use ship with toilets and power and food preparation arranged, the ability to transport large populations suddenly required us to prepare places to transport them *to*. And as with the transport ship, this suggested the need for a large offworld infrastructure we really had no way to build.

The Hyacinth were themselves busy with the ship project, but they suggested that the construction of cities was a thing all of their peers had taken on at some point, and when we put a request for bids out on the microfold we got many responses. Some effort went into evaluating these, and we visited all the finalists in the Horse Pill to size them up.

The first winning bid came from a race we had never dealt with before, so we had no human name for them. Their ancestors had been herbivorous grazers and even though the Curators had made their ancestors omnivorous they still had many features like eyes on the side of their heads and wide nostrils above a powerful jaw that we associate with grazing prey animals. They wore fur in a natural explosion of colored patterns with only the Mark of the Curators at the small of their backs being somewhat consistent between individuals. I dubbed them the Citymakers and it stuck until we started letting other city projects a few years later.

The Citymakers were offered a human fold drive in return for an empty city ready to receive five million human habitants. The city had to provide running water, power distribution, drainage, sewerage, and food production. We learned in the late going that the last item was actually possible; in addition to nanites, alien tech included techniques for growing all sorts of meat and vegetable matter in a continuous stream. The end result was suitable for preparation by the usual cooking techniques, and it could be made hard to distinguish from actual Earth food.

With nanites, such a city would take about the same amount of time to complete as the fold ship Laputa. It was a bigger project, but since it wasn't in orbit it was easier to supply the nanites with raw materials.

Our first city would be located on the fourth world M and I had claimed, which I had called Pan for its Pangea-like single continent. Like the Earth in the time of the dinosaurs it had ocean at both poles and so no ice caps, and its ocean level had been very stable for millions of years. It also had storms but these tended to be limited to its great ocean, and it had huge inland estuaries where its continent was beginning to split apart which were relatively peaceful. This gave it tens of thousands of kilometers of relatively safe shoreline on which to relocate people who were used to living near the water, but wary of the bad things that water could do.

The search for new colonies was closing; we had claimed enough worlds to meet any reasonable need, and our leaders didn't want to make it look like we were going on a march across the galaxy. This meant that the services M and I had been providing via really small ships like the old Grasshopper or the new Horse Pill weren't going to be needed much longer. While we were contemplating this our human-form Curator came to the house for barbecue, as he liked to do on Friday nights, and he slipped me a note.

"You should visit this world while you can," he said with the oddest hint of a smile.

"Can I ask why?"

"Oh you can ask, but you will only get an answer if you go there while you can."

It wasn't quite as far from Earth as Kattegat, but it was a similarly brutal journey for the average fold ship. Next time we went out on a "routine" mission we made it there in less than an hour in the Horse Pill.

We were greeted immediately. "Earth ship Horse Pill welcome to *scree*. Please follow these entry coordinates." We followed the directions, and found ourselves in a courtyard in what looked like a very old city that had originally been built by nanites, but gradually converted to more picturesque materials.

The native who greeted us on the ground was more human-looking than most of the aliens we'd met; he was mostly naked and hairless and concealed his crotch with a loincloth. He had hair on his forearms and calves but not on his head. "Don't be deceived," he said as we debarked. "I look like your hosts, but I only walk among them. My colleague sent you to us."

"You're a Curator," M said. He nodded.

THE CURATORS

"You're naturally speaking English without a translator," I added.

"Relatively easy for these people. Allow me to introduce you to their leader."

We wound our way through a city toward some kind of temple or palace complex, and we passed dozens of people all of whom seemed young and strong. Alien physiology can be deceiving but age is a thing that ravages in common ways across the galaxy, and by the time we met our host we were wondering what happened to all their old people.

"You may call me President Franklin," she said. We only knew her sex because her title declared it. The loincloth concealed her genitals and our hosts weren't mammals. "You have come a long way to meet with us. Please let us offer hospitality." That led to something like a state dinner, introductions, and much small talk. Finally the President asked the key question: "Do you know why you have been asked here?"

"Honestly, we don't," M said.

"Of course not. Our secret is not well-kept but neither is it extensively broadcast. I understand you are aware that the Curators can individually live for millions of years?"

"Yes, we know that," I said.

"We can too. I am over four million of our years old, which I believe is about six point five million of your Earth years. Of course our Curator guest is at least ten times older than I am."

"You are still among the easiest of our children to walk with," the Curator said.

"We have been asked to evaluate you. The Curators do not dispense the gift of longevity to their children, but we have been known to do that."

"Is there a price?" M asked.

"Oh no, that would be truly evil. There is an evaluation. I have to say our initial read of your species is not promising; you have overpopulated your homeworld, which is why you need colonies. The first thing you must do to be long-lived as individuals is curb your rate of reproduction. Tell me about yourselves, M and J, you are a mated pair are you not? Have you reproduced?"

We shook our heads. "It was never a priority for us," M said.

"And now you are at your species' menopause, are you not M? Do you feel loss at missing your chance to reproduce?"

"A lot of my people do, but I don't," she said. "I have given my species worlds. Childrearing would seem anticlimactic."

The President looked at me. "I couldn't have said it better," I added.

"We will need to do a fairly detailed bioassay of both of you. It will be somewhat invasive, but we need to determine which of the Curators' building blocks got included in your genome and phenotype. From that we can determine what might be possible with our technology. Subject of course to your consent."

"I don't think anybody back home would forgive us if we denied you."

"That is a poor reason to agree. Do you agree to do this for yourselves? Do you want to live longer?"

"Yes," we said almost in unison.

"Have you considered *why* you would want such a thing?"

M and I looked at one another, a bit baffled.

"You have looked beyond reproduction, for what reason do you want long life?"

"I want to know what happens next," I said, and M nodded solemnly. "I guess that sounds a bit lame."

"On the contrary, it is one of the best reasons to want long life," the President said. "The word you should probably use to name us in your language is, 'witness.' The reason that we hate death is that we hate forgetting and relearning the same lesson over and over again. Our longevity is not a privilege; it is a responsibility to observe what happens and learn from it. Be assured we are paying very close attention to what your species is doing. As a new thing it commands our attention."

We looked at the Curator, who was being very quiet.

"Our friends the Curators have their own reasons for living a long time, but their project is not ours. We are of course grateful to them for creating our world and our species. But we are watching them too."

We spent the next two days in a medical facility undergoing all manner of scans, samplings, and tests. Afterward we rested for a couple more days before we were summoned to hear the results.

"Your metabolism gave us no surprises," the top medic said. "We could make you live as long as we do."

"But we won't," the President said. M and I looked at her. "Your species has done grand things but you are still very immature. What we will give you is a modest boost." The medic offered us a wooden box. "This serum will increase your maximum life expectancy from your current seventy to a hundred to from two to three hundred of your years, and will also cure most of your worst diseases of age such as coronary disease, cancer, and most forms of dementia. It's a simple thing for us which you would almost certainly work out for yourselves within a few hundred years, but we think it would be useful for you to start learning maturity now, and it's hard to do that when you practically die in infancy. Come back to us in a few thousand years and we may be willing to help you go to another level."

"All of us alive now will be dead by then though," M said.

"Mostly so," the President agreed.

"It is still a boon," I said. "One we can use, because I think you're right about our maturity problem."

We completed our assigned tour and returned home. The serum had been designed to be replicated by nanites, so aliens were consulted to contract for that. M and I didn't need it because we had already been treated in the course of our bioassay. We went out on another tour, but within a month the Horse Pill was decommissioned to free up its fold drive for a larger ship. M and I decided to retire, and we ended up taking the Laputa to Pan to settle in the first large offworld human city, Newer Orleans.

Episode 26

We lost Miami before we had a chance to save it. While the Laputa was in early construction, hurricane Wilson came across Florida's peninsula and drove a five meter storm surge into the vulnerable city. The residential suburbs were annihilated. The city persisted as a set of tall buildings with flooded basements in the old downtown, some of which were originally residential and others of which were quickly converted. But the evacuation had not gone well and the death toll had finally dwarfed that of the Galveston hurricane of 1900. The sea was coming for many of Man's works, and Man was finally ready to take notice.

Wilson had re-strengthened after crossing Florida and made a beeline for New Orleans. There the evacuation went better, and the massive stormworks erected in the decades after Katrina did their job, if only by inches. Many of the Wilson survivors of both Miami and New Orleans never came back.

Two years later Laputa was in space trials and a furious debate was going on in Congress. Officially the human-alien program was international, but as a practical matter it was Americans who built the fold and supergravity drives and so my leaders dominated the conversation. I was officially retired, but my wife had been drafted to be chief test pilot for the Laputa and

I had of course brokered the *Pax Kattegat*. And we had taken one of the first nanite-built houses offered in Newer Orleans, leading the necessary exodus of our homeworld.

The sea was also coming for a hundred other human cities. It was flooding the understory of lower Manhattan every few years, and since preventing the seawater incursion had proven impossible drastic measures had been taken to make the underground recoverable in the aftermath, with everything except the subway tracks moved above the floodline where possible. Flood insurance had become impossible to obtain for anything on a barrier island or beach anywhere in the world, and millions of dwellings were either snapped up by the wealthy or abandoned depending on their circumstances.

When Laputa landed in Newfoundland it was an event of galactic importance. It was the largest starship ever to make landfall in all the billions of years the galaxy had been gardened by the Curators. The Hyacinth actually waited for us to land Laputa before attempting to do the same with their twin ship. Nothing like trusting the other guys' engineering.

Then the decision was made that the city to evacuate first had to be New Orleans, but you couldn't land such a massive thing on the soft swampland surrounding the city. It was M who noted that the supergravity drive used the same amount of energy no matter what its field radius was, so it took only the charge from a couple of car batteries to levitate the ship for weeks at a time. So like an object out of an Arthur C. Clarke novel the Laputa appeared above the swamp south of New Orleans, and floating vehicles began what would become the largest planetary evacuation in galactic history.

The Laputa would be joined within ten years by the Pandora and the Galactica. We built a new facility for making fold drives and recruited five more species to help us building offworld cities. It took twenty years but we managed to move half our population offworld without any more catastrophes like Miami, even though Earth's seas continued to rise and their storms became ever stronger and more frequent.

The Consortium which the Hyacinth had started eventually became pretty proficient at making supergravity drives, although their yield never got better than eighty percent or so while ours on earth was over ninety-nine percent. While we evacuated the Earth it became apparent over the microfold that all over the galaxy, worlds were taking a wait-and-see attitude before starting new capital fold ship projects. With the demonstration of Laputa and the understanding that something the size of a baseball made it possible to land such a thing instead of keeping it in orbit, nobody wanted to waste the resources making an old style fold ship if they weren't sure it wouldn't soon be obsolete.

Out in the galaxy the economic value of human-made fold drives, which were a hundred times harder to make than supergravity drives, wasn't based on their small size; it was their nearly perfect calibration, which made it possible to fold across the galaxy in a single operation and actually arrive at your target. This was a fortunate thing because we had a lot of cities to build on our colonies fast and many species were eager to trade resources to get one of those drives. And while the cities they built all incorporated human architectural motifs they also all brought in a bit of their own, so the colony worlds took on personalities according to both the human source culture and the aliens who had helped us build them. It made for more of a tourist industry than we had ever expected to sustain, and it was the small Earth fold ships still the size of airliners that made that trade possible.

And the Witness serum had all but eliminated human death. There were still tragic exceptions, but they were tragic *because* they were exceptions. There had been some discussion of keeping the serum secret or limiting its distribution, but some person whose initial might have been M or J might have had something to do with publicizing its existence. In previous circumstances it might have devastated the foundations of our economy, but in the midst of the planetary evacuation it made no real difference regarding anything except that people who would have died continued to live.

But the Witness serum had its limits, and futures were trading higher in the tattered remnants of the human funeral industry as we all got older. Forty years later, as I marked my ninetieth birthday, my doctor showed me a graph. "I want you to see this first," he said. "This is my response to the collagen cross-linking test since I took the serum." It rose gradually across the decades, signaling that there were some things the serum couldn't fix.

"Now you may have been wondering why you and, I suppose M, look so young. This is yours." The same graph started flat and stayed flat, not rising a pixel across decades of sampling.

"So what does that mean?"

"It means something is fixing your collagen. As far as we know nothing can *stop* it from cross-linking. That would be a breakthrough."

"That's very funny," I said.

"There's nothing funny about it. You might want to come clean with us about what else was done to you."

When I got home M and our human-form Curator friend were waiting. "You're busted," the Curator said. "You need to get back to the Witnesses before your own people get to you. There is a ship in orbit about to debark, and I can get you there before anyone knows. Unfortunately I don't have the amplifier belt, so I can't get you any further than that ship on my own, and I'm very much on my own at the moment."

"Busted for *what?*" I asked.

"Obviously you got more than just the boost serum. Some Curator might have slipped the Witnesses a suggestion about that. But now you need to find out just what they really did so you can figure out what to do about it."

We folded to the starship moments before our front door was broken down. On the alien starship we were just human hangers-on, metabolism type 23, showed up mysteriously but to the aliens your mere presence, however unexplainable, indicated the right to air, quarters, food, privacy, and transport to your next destination if there was a ship going that way.

Our first journey to visit to the Witnesses in the Horse Pill had taken less than an hour. Taking regularly scheduled galactic transports, with the usual turnaround times between each leg, our return was going to take at least a year.

Episode 27

On the alien ship our Curator showed us how to claim quarters. First we needed a key, which we had to have made. Aliens didn't like using direct biometrics for every access request, but they did verify that nobody with my geneprint had already claimed a key aboard the ship. Then with the key we could claim a cabin, occupancy two, metabolism type 23. We did all this through a touchscreen terminal with what humans would consider intolerable user interface latency.

In the end we got entry to a forty cubic meter stateroom whose amenities, along with the nearby services, would be mostly compatible with our biological functions. We were scheduled to fold out in eight hours.

We were no longer in the world of quaintly named worlds and ships. We had fortunately taught ourselves the trading language the aliens call Common so it was possible for us to pass. There were four spoken versions of Common meant to accommodate different vocal capabilities, and the idea was that you learned to understand all four but spoke the one best suited to your species. Like the human trading language Swahili Common wasn't a language meant for epic poetry, but it allowed vastly different individuals to communicate when translation services weren't available. And away from Earth, translation services were reserved for official use and special occasions, because they involved microfold communication to a world with enough computational resources to perform them.

And everything was done numerically, starting by reference to worlds on the Curator's Index. We were on our way to world CI:827490, about forty light-years from Earth. Our ship was the thirty-ninth built and operated by the natives of world CI:627960, so it was ship 627960:39. Humans had built so many tiny ships that the nomenclature had broken down in our case, but we were leaving the part of the galaxy where that would be important for awhile.

"You need to conceal yourselves," the Curator said. "Your human habits will betray you, and I think they can track our personal folds now well enough to eventually figure out where I took you. They will then know where you are going on this leg of your journey."

This filled me with panic, but M just said "Let me make a list of some supplies we will need."

We hid in the stateroom while the Curator folded down to the Earth and then, about an hour later, reappeared. "This is everything you asked for, plus two tablet computers and common-compatible power bricks. I have prepped them with the entire Curator Index and a full table of regularly scheduled transports. This should give you everything you need to find your way to the Witnesses. Be careful not to reveal these machines' true capabilities, as that will reveal your origin."

The Curator showed us several other useful things, such as how to get the ship informational displays to show all the fold ships present in our system. "If they come after you they will not be able to conceal it," he said. "Although it will be a bit tricky for you to evade them using regularly scheduled transports. I will alert our agents that you are coming, in case they can help."

"I never quite saw this being how I would start my ninth decade," I said after he left.

"I don't think either of us ever saw either of us seeing a ninth decade," M said. "The world was in big trouble, and people our age tended to die of cancer or end up in nursing homes instead of being indistinguishable from children in their twenties. I'm not going to complain."

"It's our own people we are running from. They have the best technology."

"This is true. But I am a warrior, you are a diplomat, and we are both human too."

"So what's the plan?"

She dumped out the bag the Curator had brought us. It was filled with body paint and a hair trimmer kit. "What do off-worlders know about humans? We wear clothes and we have hair on our heads and no Mark of the Curators. So we will invert all those things." She opened up the haircut kit and handed me the electric trimmer. "You'll have to do me," she said.

"You want me to cut off your hair?"

"Oh, I'm going to follow up by cutting off all of yours. Even..." She glanced significantly at my crotch. "We are going to play much hairier beings than we really are that ritually shaved ourselves, thus explaining our current total nakedness. And then painted up of course, thanks to the raiders for teaching us that art."

The last part of the disguise was, of course, the Mark, which she put at the small of our backs. "It's not very convincing, so our story will be that it's in differently colored hair when we're not shaved," M advised.

"Usually when the Mark is in fur color, there are also skin differences."

"Yes, but the body paint would hide those, and I think most observers will casually assume that we traced them."

When we were properly made up we left the room to find typical alien travel bags, which were of course free for the taking at a convenient dispensary. We found a disposal and got rid of our Earth clothes. We kept a few Earth ID items and the tablets in our kits, which we wore over the shoulder in a fashion that had been common throughout the galaxy since long before our own ancestors learned to use fire.

After the ship folded we waited a couple of hours and then checked the system status display. It showed a human foldship had entered the system mere minutes after our ship had.

When we got back to the cabin, it was occupied. Our visitor was tall and covered in thick, dark fur. Her Mark of the Curators was bleached white on her chest, where a human female's breasts would be.

"Let me guess, you walk among these folks," I said as we entered.

"Good guess," she said in perfect English. "My colleague said you were in trouble. Easy to see how."

"And you saw right through our disguises," I said.

"Oh, that's just us," she said brightly. "I can see your genomic structure as clearly as you can see skin color. You're definitely human. But most of our children will look right past you unless they have been studying Earth pornography."

"Right now we have what you call a shell game to play. There are three regular trade foldships including this one in orbit here. They are all traditional form so none of them can land, and all depend on orbital transports. And then there are your people, who can land, but can't dock with the other two ships. Since it visits Earth regularly they can dock with this one. Which means..." She offered her hands.

"Are we safe now?" M asked after we got a cabin on the new foldship.

"Not really. They have several days and while our information systems don't record the wealth of data yours do, if they are thorough—and our experience is that humans can be remarkably thorough—they will interview enough passengers to learn of the odd couple that fits no known pattern. I'm not sure if their single ship could detect or track my fold activity. So they will know you are on one of these three ships, and if necessary they can deploy teams to follow all three to their destinations."

"This is hopeless," I said thudding my head against the wall behind me.

"If it was hopeless I wouldn't be here," the Curator said. "We didn't populate the galaxy by doing hopeless."

"What do we do then?"

"Keep doing what you are doing. I am contacting our agents on the world where this ship is going. You will not be alone."

But then she disappeared. "I hope that means she knows they can't track her," I said.

"Let's adjust our disguises," M said more helpfully.

After we folded there were soon two human foldships in the new system. I consulted the tablet and found we'd also gone ten light years in the wrong direction to get where we wanted to be. This being pursued thing would not do.

Our new Curator liaison was feathered, very much like the Hyacinth but with a more mammalian toothy mouth and dark grey feathers. It spoke in the Common dialect we call clacky. "Your pursuers are dangerously close," it said seriously.

"Obvious," M replied in the more human friendly soft dialect.

"This has to conclude. Fortunately our leaders have finally concurred. Please." It offered us its wing foreclaws, and when we took them we were treated to a dizzying flash of world after world as we folded over and over again, finally settling in the familiar palace courtyard of the Witnesses.

Before we could voice the question, our host opened its tunic to reveal an amplifier belt. "Your home Curator convinced our leaders that we had created your trouble, and so we had an obligation," it said. "Nothing in the galaxy could follow us now. And we are told that your people do not know of this place."

"We are mostly sure of that," M said.

"I have alerted your hosts, and they are waiting for you," it said.

What we did not know at that time was that our superiors were doing a fine computer analysis of the fold logs from the Horse Pill. It hadn't been tracked to the Witnesses by any known entity, but it had kept its own tracking log of what it had done.

Following those forty year old logs across thousands of light-years was a nontrivial task, but they had put some of the best engineers on Earth on the job of tracing our steps. And so the people chasing us did in due course figure out the Curator's Index of the Witnesses' world.

Episode 28

The President of the Witnesses looked exactly as she had forty years previously. M and I did not—we looked very noticeably younger and healthier, despite our advanced age. And this was a problem because the boost serum they had given humanity doesn't reverse most of the hazards of already being old, it only slows down further aging.

We were naked and in body paint so as to hide our identity on our travels. "Welcome back," the President said. "We expected to see you again, but not quite so soon. I realize this is not how you would choose to present yourselves to others. We have quarters and clothing for you if you would like to adjust your appearance."

"That would be nice," M said.

In our private room clothes were laid out for us upon a much more Earthlike bed than we had been assigned on our first visit. After washing off the body paint we looked at the clothes and M said, "these appear to be just like the outfits we were wearing on our last visit."

"Not duplicates though," I pointed out. "More like reproductions. They are made with natural fibers, I don't think you can do that with nanites."

When we returned to the conference room there was a buffet of very convincing Earthlike food. We nibbled and sat with the leaders of the Witnesses and the feathered Curator who had brought us to them. "To begin we owe you an apology," the President said. "We could not resist the temptation to test our biological understanding on beings who do not have any of the thirty-five known genetic triggers that create the Mark of the Curator in various species."

"You made us immortal?" I asked.

"None of us is immortal," she said. "We don't age and we heal very well. You will find that you can last a very long time without oxygen and you will regenerate limbs and nerve damage that you couldn't before. But enough trauma done quickly enough, particularly to the brain, will kill any of us."

"Barring that, how long can we expect to live?" M asked.

"We honestly can't say. The boost, which we give to any species that asks for it, is generic to your individual members once we tailor it to your species. It mostly corrects things that are easy to correct, but which evolution doesn't bother to. The Cure, which provides for longer life, is much more individually specific. On the long term there are thousands of more subtle equilibria which must be stabilized and sources of damage to repair. We would have advised you to return in forty or fifty thousand years for a checkup, after which we could give you a clearer longer-term picture. With such a checkup I think we could guarantee several hundred thousand years, and depending on certain tests would more likely suggest between two and three million as a likely target. Further checkups might extend even that."

"I don't think we have any idea how to thank you," I said.

"You shouldn't thank us. We did it to you without warning and we know it isn't unheard of for those who haven't received our gifts to capture and dissect those who have to try unlocking our secrets. We did it because you are the only living beings who have ever seen a planet folded into its star, and because each of you has also accomplished something famous, victory in rare foldship battle and brokering the most unlikely peace accord the Galaxy has seen in aeons. Our motives were selfish and we should have at least told you what we were doing."

"Do the people who dissect your beneficiaries ever get what they are looking for?"

"No, which is the most annoying thing about that. As with your fold drives, there really isn't any secret to the Cure, except a long period of learning and building specialized machinery and a lot of hard work which must be executed perfectly to make use of that knowledge. The cellular mechanisms we inserted into your bodies are tuned for your individual genotypes and any one of them will only work for a small fraction of other beings, even of your own species. Our library of such tweaks and our understanding of how to deploy them is vast though. We were mildly suprised not to find any surprises in your genome related to your lack of the Mark."

"These clothes seem to be replicas of what we wore on our last visit," M said.

"Ah, yes. So they are. It is our mission to witness what we can, so we examined your clothing while we were working on your bodies, and found it a fascinating source of mystery. Your clothes were made of a mix of natural and synthetic fibers assembled somehow to be much tougher and more durable than anything we could make for ourselves, if we needed such material. We sought to learn your techniques for reference." She dialed a code on a touchpad, and had a brief conversation in a very nonhuman language. "Let me introduce you to our fabric researcher."

We took a brief ride on a hover scooter through palace halls and courtyards and came to a large room filled with fabric samples. A male Witness approached and said, in less natural but perfectly understandable English, "Welcome to the textile lab."

We bowed. "Are these samples from all over the galaxy?" M asked.

"No. These are all from Earth. No other world makes fabric such as humans do." He led us past rows of samples of silk, cotton, synthetics, and blends to a loom. "Even with your open historical records, it took us five years to build a machine which could theoretically do industrial production of cloth such as you were doing four hundred Earth years ago, before you even had electricity. Nanites are remarkably unhelpful in building a loom."

"Why do you take such interest in this?" M asked.

"We think it made you what you are. Everybody is so impressed with your fold drives—and make no mistake, they are impressive—that they lose the thread of where your ability to make such things came from. And we find in your modesty habit and your insatiable need for cloth the thing that drove your first quest to make a really complex machine despite your lack of nanite technology. Some speak of your aggressiveness and talent for war, but you were still making weapons by handicraft when you were making textiles by industrial techniques. It would be over a hundred years into your industrial revolution

THE CURATORS 193

before you learned to make firearms as well as you could make cloth."

While we were thinking of that a loudspeaker broadcast something in what we had come to assume was the Witnesses' own language. "We should go back to the conference room," the President said. "Your pursuers have found you."

"We have come from Earth to recover two human fugitives. We have reason to believe they might have come to this world. We have the ability to land on any small flat place, please advise."

The President looked at us, and pressed a touch button. "Why do you seek these fugitives," she asked.

"They are dangerous. Their presence on your world places you in great jeopardy."

"For reference, this is a smile," she said to us, flashing what we as humans would call something like a grimace. Then she hit the touchpad. "Landing directions are forthcoming." She touched another point. "Guide the Earth ship to our north courtyard, then make sure they can't leave."

"They are the violent ones," M said.

"We know."

Half an hour later the other humans stomped into the room, carrying J20 combat firearms. "So nice of you to hold them for us," their leader said with a sneer.

"Oh we didn't hold them for you. We used them as bait."

M and I looked at one another.

The other humans raised their rifles but stopped half-way and collapsed twitching. "Your real reason for coming here is that you want our technology. Too bad that technology makes it so simple to synthesize a paralytic to target your genome," the President said.

"Wait, if your paralytic targets humans, why are we still upright?" M asked.

"Well, one of the other things we neglected to warn you about is that after the Cure, you aren't *exactly* human any more. There are some who feel that the Cure destroys the individual, changing them into a new and alien being. It does make you sterile by design, but you had already forgone reproduction within your natural window for that."

"But you did it to us even though some people feel that way about it?"

"Those people are idiots, and you didn't strike us as being that stupid." She gestured toward our now fully immobile pursuers. "Put these lot to sleep and process them. M, you are familiar with Earth technology, would you do us the favor of giving their ship a look-over?"

"With pleasure," she said.

Episode 29

While the Witnesses did whatever it is they do to those who try to steal their secrets, we made our way to our pursuers' ship with the Curator and a couple of Witness technicians. It had been painted black, but their ship looked *awfully* familiar.

"Tell me this isn't the *Horse Pill*," I said as we walked up.

"Not sure," M said. "Biometric entry pad would be new. But if it's our ship..." She traced down from the keypad and found a small recessed panel, which she gave a sharp whack. The door popped open.

"It's the *Horse Pill*," she said. "We never had much use for security and most of the places we went getting locked out was a bigger problem. There's an impact switch hidden there. They obviously missed it when they refitted it."

"Where the hell did they find a fold drive?"

"That's a good question. I personally removed serial number 122 and helped install it in the Trinity class *Ajax*."

Inside the ship the fold drive console was buzzing frantically and the display background had turned red. "That doesn't look good," M said as she tried the controls. Everything was frozen. It wasn't even clear how to enter a pass code to get access.

"The lockout could be any stupid thing," M said. "These guys obviously like their secrets." The console let out five long blasts and began flashing.

"Fold activity," the Curator said.

"Well we're still here. If it's trying to fold, why is it not succeeding?"

"We operate a fold inhibitor," one of the Witness techs said.

"REALLY," M said. "A member of a certain elder race once told *us* they would destroy it if we had put an inhibitor online."

"The Witnesses shutter it for us. It takes three to four hundred milliseconds to form a fold, and the inhibitor is only open for about a hundred and thirty milliseconds per window. If you don't know the schedule, you can't get through. Oh, and this thing is retrying about every eight seconds."

"Let's see if they bothered to hide the diagnostic tools." She went to a panel and rapped it; like the one outside the ship it popped open. "Fucking amateurs," she said. She turned the hidden display on and a dense list of control codes began scrolling by. She paused it a few times and said, "What the hell."

"What is it?"

"We need to pull the floor. Like right now." There was a toolbag inside the panel beneath the display. It contained a utility knife, which we used to cut the rubber flooring so we could fold it out of the way, and a security screwdriver which fitted the recessed screws around a metal floor plate. A few minutes later we were looking down at a silver sphere about half a meter across which was cradled in a nest of spring-loaded electrodes. M pulled a lever on its arm and the largest visible electrode, right at the top, popped up and away. At this point the pilot's console protested one last time and crashed out to a command prompt.

"Didn't think of that one, did you fuckers." M went back to the console and tapped a few commands into the interface.

"You remember how to work all this stuff after all these years?" I asked, not ironically.

"Like riding a bicycle," she said. "I *designed* this control protocol." She looked at a couple of readings, then what looked like a couple of file dumps, then at a couple of other things a bit more frantically. "This isn't possible," she finally said.

"What isn't..." But she had already turned and blown past me, and started releasing the electrode holders around the spherical fold drive. When it was free she asked for me to help her. "Fucking thing masses sixty kilograms," she said, and at her direction I helped her turn it over. On what had been its side was an area of engraved symbols. The most prominent said *S/N 0104*. When M saw it she collapsed on her haunches, as if the air had been let out from her.

"It's one of the eight, isn't it?" I asked. She nodded gravely.

"The eight what?" one of the Witness techs asked.

"The first eight fold drives the humans made were capable of being detuned," the Curator explained. "They were supposed to be destroyed after the event M and J here witnessed where a world was folded into its sun by that mechanism."

"So? Every fold drive can be detuned. It's why we have the inhibitor."

"Ours are small, and they can be remotely controlled," I said. "Notice nobody was here to operate it. Was it trying to fold the world away? It wasn't just trying to hide itself?"

"It was scrambling the prime calibration constant. New drives won't take anything out of a narrow range we know to be safe. There is only one reason for the drive console to send such a command to the sphere." She went to the console and sat down. "Fortunately everything these assholes know about computer security could be written on a grain of sand in 24 point type. I'll need a human-made portable data drive and tablet. With these idiots, we can probably find both on board."

Four days later we watched as our pursuers were led into a meeting, wearing short sleeved white robes. We had had a bit of an argument with the Witnesses about what to call this affair; they insisted that trial, inquest, and hearing were all wrong. But they couldn't tell us an English word for it that was *right*.

"Human Q," the Witness running the affair finally said, "you and your associates have been caught pursuing for capture those who have received our gifts, and leaving a trap upon our world which attempted to destroy the entire planet. Now you will learn our response."

"We don't get a plea or a defense?"

"No. I believe your fellow humans do have questions for you."

"So where did you get the fold drive?" M asked sweetly.

"I got a big asshole," the leader 'Q' said. "Just popped out one day."

I pulled the cover cloth that was concealing the fold drive on a stand next to us. "Does your asshole have serial number 104?" I asked.

"Okay, you're good," Q admitted. "But fuck you. One day the people who sent me will get you anyway. Are you really stupid enough to think we would destroy something as valuable as a *fold drive* just because you don't like what else can be done with it?"

"Well we did destroy an awful lot of nuclear weapons. And I'm guessing some of the people who sent you diverted this. Back on Earth there will be a hearing and an inquiry and I bet a trial."

Q shrugged.

"If the people who sent you don't capture and dissect you first," the leading Witness said. We all looked at her.

"And why would they do that," Q asked evenly.

"Because we gave you what you came here for. We don't believe in violence ourselves, but we reasoned that it would only be just to make you live with the same kind of nuisance we foisted on our guests. We will of course make sure that all the official channels on Earth are aware of what happened here and what we have done."

"You made them *immortal*?!" I yelled a bit undiplomatically.

"None of us is immortal," the Witness said, and I slapped my own forehead.

"We will need our stuff and our ship then," Q said.

"We have confiscated your possessions. We will let you keep these robes in furtherance of your known modesty habit. You will board the next fold transport to *screee*. We will give you a comfortable head start to travel elsewhere from there before we let your employers know what is going on."

Q looked squarely at M and me. "I will personally kill you both," he said.

"You were going to do that anyway," M said. "How's that working out so far?"

Later the President entertained us with her world's best distilled spirits and snacks. "I'm surprised Q didn't lunge for me across the room," M said as she ate something that had once been an actual animal and not nanite ooze.

"We reserved a mechanism to remotely paralyze and torture them," the President said as if this was the most normal thing ever. "It will wear away with disuse once they leave our influence, but they learned that obedience is best while they are our guests."

"And what about us?"

"Well we had no reason to implant discipline mechanisms in you."

"No, I mean what are we to do? We'll probably end up on the same ship with those assholes."

"We were thinking otherwise. There is after all an unclaimed and operable human vessel available. We were thinking of giving it to you."

"The fold drive is..."

"...just like every other fold drive in the galaxy," she completed for me. "I cannot think of two beings I would trust more with it. And to observe the condition we would place on our gift."

"What condition?"

"We would not attempt to impose, but just to ask. As you know we believe the purpose of life is to witness. I suppose you will find it uncomfortable to revisit your own species for some time, but there is a large galaxy out there full of life. Take your ship and witness it for us. Come back once in awhile and tell us stories about what you have seen."

"That's a good offer," M said as she threw back a shot of the liquor. "Offhand, I would like to ask for two other things."

"Please."

"First, we have to repaint the goddamn ship. I am not going to fly a black ship."

"We can accommodate that. We might have to get appropriate coatings from Earth, but we can arrange to do that discreetly. What else do you request?"

"If we are going to be traveling the galaxy, both our clothing and our bare skin will stand out. Could you use your technology to give us fur?"

"Very easily," she said.

About the Author

Roger Williams is the author of the cult classic, **The Metamorphosis of Prime Intellect.** Find out more on his official author website, localroger.com.

Printed in Great Britain
by Amazon